DEATH RIDES A PINTO

Egan Blue is small in stature, speaks softly, is polite, and might be taken for a schoolteacher — but for the well-worn gun on his hip. Knowing he hasn't got long to live, Blue sets about cleaning up the West, one killer at a time. That's what brings him to San Dimas, where the local ranchers are being terrorized by masked night riders, and the town council is willing to pay any price to get rid of them.

STEVE HAYES

DEATH RIDES
A PINTO

Complete and Unabridged

LINFORD
Leicester

First published in Great Britain in 2015

First Linford Edition
published 2017

A catalogue record for this book is available
from the British Library.

ISBN 978–1–4448–3340–9

Published by
F. A. Thorpe (Publishing)
Anstey, Leicestershire

Set by Words & Graphics Ltd.
Anstey, Leicestershire
Printed and bound in Great Britain by
T. J. International Ltd., Padstow, Cornwall

This book is printed on acid-free paper

Prologue

Atlanta, 1864

The elegant mansion, with its stately marble columns and red brick steps leading up to a front door bearing the family crest, was already in flames. Smoke poured from the broken windows and part of its roof had caved in.

Inside, Union soldiers, their faces blackened by smoke, laughingly used a majestic grand piano as a battering ram to smash open the French windows. They then carried the piano to a bonfire already burning on the spacious green lawn. There, urged on by three smirking officers watching from horseback, the soldiers threw the piano onto the fire and then danced in devilish glee as it soon became engulfed in flames.

Nearby, an eight-year-old boy, dressed

1

in red velvet and silk, his girlishly-long blond hair black with soot, sobbed as he watched his mother and father dragged by soldiers to a recently dug pit in the once-beautiful rose-garden. There, prodded into position by bayonets, his parents stood with their backs to the pit, while other soldiers herded their son in front of them.

'All right now, boy,' a sergeant said, forcing a cocked Remington Army revolver into his hand. 'Here's your chance to save either your ma or pa. It's up to you — ' He paused as two soldiers approached, each with a copperhead wriggling on the end of a stick. Waiting for them to toss the deadly snakes into the pit and back away, he then turned back to the boy, saying: 'Whichever one you wants to live, you got to shoot the other. Don't you dare defy me, boy,' he snarled as the boy vehemently shook his head. 'You don't do as I say, I'll have my men kill 'em both. And believe me, they won't do it quick. They'll take their own sweet time, sticking 'em like hogs till they bleed to death!'

The boy sobbed even harder, but still didn't raise the revolver at his side.

'Watkins, Hastings!' The sergeant beckoned to two soldiers. 'Put your steel into that no-good southern bitch!'

'N-No!' the boy screamed as the soldiers started toward his mother.

'Hold it,' the sergeant ordered. Then to the boy: 'Get on with it, you sniveling little bastard.'

Shaking with fear, the boy raised the gun and tried to aim it at his folks. He couldn't. Still sobbing, he dropped the revolver and ran. But immediately several soldiers blocked his way, threatening him with their bayonets, allowing the sergeant to grab him and force him to face his parents.

'Thought I was funning with you, huh?' he said to the boy. 'Well, let me show you what real fun is. I'll make you laugh till your sides split! All right,' he yelled at the soldiers. 'Go to work on 'em!'

The soldiers charged at the boy's parents.

But before they reached them, the father took matters into his own hands.

'If one of us has to die,' he shouted, 'let it be me!' Quickly kissing his wife on the cheek, he whispered something only she heard then turned and jumped into the pit.

Instantly, the copperheads attacked him.

His wife screamed and buried her face in her hands.

The boy tried to twist free of the sergeant's grip. But the man was too strong for him. Holding him with one hand, he signaled to his men with the other.

'Well, what're you waiting for? Enjoy yourselves, boys!'

Grinning, the soldiers raised their rifles and fired point-blank at the wife, who staggered back and fell into the pit beside her dying husband.

Horrified, the boy cried out in despair. Then, eyes bright with hate, he sank his teeth into the sergeant's hand. As the man yelped and jerked his hand away, the boy broke free and ran to the edge of the pit.

He looked down and saw that both his parents were dead.

In a state of shock he watched the copperheads wriggling away. Then rage replaced his despair and whirling around, he ran to the gun that still lay where he'd dropped it. Picking it up he held it with both hands, aimed it at the sergeant and fired.

The .44 caliber steel-jacket bullet, a newcomer to the Civil War, punched a hole in the sergeant's chest. He staggered back, his expression one of disbelief as he realized the boy had shot him. Then he crumpled sideways, hit the ground and unable to stop himself rolled into the pit.

The boy heard the sergeant's scream as the copperheads buried their poisonous fangs into him. He shuddered, but at the same time felt a sense of satisfaction knowing that the man who'd ordered his folks' death was now dead himself.

It did not make up for his loss . . . but it helped.

It also shaped his character for the rest of his life.

1

(New Mexico – 1888)

The two belligerent gunmen at the bar in the Long Creek saloon were drunk. Under ordinary circumstances the bartender, a large hulking man named Buck Willis, would have refused to serve them or grabbed his shotgun and ordered them to get out.

But these weren't ordinary circumstances, because these weren't ordinary drunks. Identical twin brothers, the Dixons not only looked alike but had identical personalities. Both were ill-tempered with mean streaks that became worse when fueled by whisky. They were happiest when hurting or bullying someone, men or women, and were fast enough on the draw to make any lawman think twice before challenging them.

Tonight, they were drunk and itching to kill anyone who gave them trouble. Willis, who knew the Dixons well, recognized the warning signs and had no intention of getting shot for trying to be a hero. Instead, he signaled with his eyes to the other customers that it was time they left. As a result, one by one the locals quickly finished their drinks, said goodnight and scampered out like frightened mice.

Morgan Dixon, the elder brother by two minutes, eventually caught on to what was happening. He immediately drew his six-gun and warned the last three customers that he'd shoot the next man who tried to leave.

The customers paled but remained at the bar.

'Give 'em another drink,' Morgan told Willis. 'Can't you see they're thirsty?'

Willis quickly poured three whiskies and set them before the customers.

'Leave it,' snarled Morgan as the bartender started to take the bottle away. 'My pals and me, we're going to drink it dry 'fore this night's over.'

Willis left the bottle on the bar and stepped back. In front of him beneath the bar was a sawed-off shotgun that he only used as a last resort. He was tempted to use it now on the Dixon brothers but lost his nerve.

Ian Knapp had more guts. 'No, thanks, mister,' he told Morgan, 'I've had enough to drink.' He turned to leave then jumped, startled, as Hoag Dixon drew and fired his Colt .45 at the bottle, shattering it, so that broken glass and whisky showered over Knapp.

'I'll put the next one through your Adam's apple,' Hoag warned the shaken barber. 'Now do like my brother says and swallow that goddamn drink!'

Knapp quickly gulped down his whisky.

'Bring us another damn bottle and bring it fast,' Hoag growled at Willis.

''Fore you do that, bartender,' a voice said quietly, 'I'd like a drink myself.'

Everyone turned and looked at the

small, slim, blond-haired man standing at the end of the bar. No one had seen or heard him enter. Though in his early thirties, he had the face of a choirboy and at first glance seemed unassuming — until one noticed his eyes. Deep-set and blue as a mountain lake, they stared out from under blond eyebrows with a strange mixture of innocence, menace and sadness.

It was the same with his smile. Pleasantly appealing to the ladies, with a hint of melancholy, it possessed a deadliness that only a fool would have dared to arouse.

Morgan chose to be that fool. Elbowing everyone aside, he confronted the blond-haired man and stabbed a finger in his face. 'Goddammit, who the hell do you think you are, butting in on my brother like that?'

'Just a man who wants a drink,' the blond-haired man replied. He spoke softly, barely above a whisper, with an educated southern drawl. Though small, there was a graceful elegance about him that commanded attention. Tanned from a life outdoors, he was dressed entirely in sun-faded blue denim and wore a blue silk kerchief around his neck. The kerchief wasn't knotted, as was customary; instead both ends were tucked through a gold signet ring bearing the same family crest — a blue falcon perched on an iron fist — that had adorned the mansion door. His boots were hand-tooled and the blue-gray flat-crowned Stetson pushed back off his head looked as if it had just come out of a box. Holstered on his left hip was a blue-steel, single-action .44 caliber Merwin Hulbert revolver. Custom-made, it had a 5-inch barrel without a sight, a turned-down hammer for faster cocking, a setback trigger and a rounded bird's head handle with polished walnut grips. Like the man, the gun commanded attention.

'A drink, huh?' Morgan grinned at his brother. 'Hear that, Hoag? This little squirt wants himself a drink.'

'Let's give him one,' said Hoag. He picked up the brass spittoon and confronted the blond-haired man. 'Here you go, mister. Drink this.'

The blond-haired man smiled, as if amused by Hoag's remark, and took the spittoon.

Everyone in the bar stared at him, waiting to see if he'd really drink from it.

The blond haired man raised the spittoon as if to drink and then, in the same motion, dumped the contents over Hoag.

The saloon went deathly quiet.

Hoag stood there, spittle and tobacco juice running down his face and chest, as stunned as everyone else.

Then with an enraged roar, he went for his gun.

His brother did the same.

The blond-haired man barely moved, or maybe he moved so fast no one noticed it, but his gun seemed to leap into his hand and he fanned it, twice.

The Dixon brothers froze in mid-motion, guns still in their holsters, each with an astonished look on his face. Each with a bullet in his heart.

For one infinitesimal moment time seemed to stop.

Then the brothers crumpled to the floor, dead, their blood staining the sawdust.

The blond-haired man looked at them dispassionately. He then calmly holstered his gun and turned to the bartender.

'I'll take that drink now, if you please.'

'Yes sir, coming right up!' Willis happily poured his finest whisky into a tumbler and set it before the blond-haired man. 'No, no,' he said as the man reached for money. 'This be on the house, mister. This . . . and as many more as you want!'

'Thanks, but I always pay my way.' The blond-haired man politely placed a silver dollar on the bar, downed the whisky and walked out.

2

Sheriff Gil Henson sat at his desk, sorting through a pile of Wanted posters. He was a big man who always looked worried, as if expecting bad news at any minute. He looked up as the door of his office opened, fearing the worst, and was relieved when he saw that the slightly built blond-haired man who'd just entered looked harmless.

'Yes, mister, what can I do for you?'

'My name's Egan Blue,' the man said softly. 'I feel obliged to tell you that I just gunned down two men in the saloon 'cross the street.'

It was said so matter-of-factly, so politely that the sheriff barely reacted.

'So those *were* shots I heard,' he said. 'I wasn't sure.'

Blue didn't say anything. He didn't have to. His cold, contemptuous stare

14

told the lawman that he was a lying coward.

Normally that wouldn't have bothered Gil Henson. He'd never pretended to be brave and was used to brushing off insults. But there was such contempt in this man's eyes, the sheriff squirmed in his chair.

'These men,' he said, with as much authority as he could muster, 'who were they, Mr. Blue?'

'Morgan and Hoag Dixon.'

The sheriff gaped, barely able to believe his ears.

'Y-You mean the Dixon brothers?'

Blue nodded.

'W-Where're the others?'

'Others?'

'The men who backed you up?'

'No one backed me up.'

Instant respect entered the lawman's eyes.

'Well, now,' he said jovially, 'ain't you the bearer of good news.'

Blue, tired of the lawman's ingratiating manner, turned to leave.

'Hold on, mister.'

Blue paused and faced the sheriff.

'This shooting . . . was it in self-defense?'

'They drew first, if that's what you mean.'

'Then it *was* self-defense?'

Blue didn't respond.

Rising, the sheriff came around the desk, hand extended, towering over Blue.

'I'd like to shake your hand, mister.'

'What for?'

'Ridding the world of a menace.'

Blue didn't answer. He stood there, looking up at this weak excuse for a lawman, and made no attempt to shake hands.

Sheriff Henson reddened, angered by the insult, and lowered his hand. 'There's a reward for the Dixons in Texas,' he said gruffly. 'I don't know how much it is but if you'll stick around I'll wire the marshal's office in El Paso and have 'em send — ' He stopped as Blue shook his head. 'What?' he added.

'You don't want it?'

'I've already been paid,' Blue said.

'Who by?'

Blue didn't say anything.

'I asked you a question, mister.'

'Ask another.'

'Not till you answer this one.'

Blue said, deadly soft: 'I can't. My client wishes to remain anonymous. He was very specific about that in the contract I signed when he paid me to kill them.'

'*Paid* you?'

'Yes.'

'How much?'

'Enough.' Blue took out a sealed envelope and placed it on the desk. 'This will cover their burials.'

Sheriff Henson frowned. 'I don't get it. Why're you wasting money on those two weasels?'

'I'm not. My client is.'

'Why?'

'It's in the contract.'

'Contract?'

Blue nodded.

Rather than prod him for an answer, the sheriff said: 'Why'd he want them dead?'

'He never said.'

'And you never asked?'

Blue didn't respond.

'I suppose *that* was in the contract, too, huh?'

Blue ignored the lawman's sarcasm.

Pissed but wary of a man capable of killing the Dixons, the sheriff said: 'Mister, who the hell are you — some kind of fancy-Jack detective or Pinkerton agent?'

'Neither.'

'Then why did this 'client' come to you?'

'It's what I do.'

'What is what you do?'

'I kill men who deserve to be killed. For a price.'

'That's murder.'

'Not if they draw first,' said Blue. 'And I make sure the men I kill always draw first.' He smiled, a pleasant yet chilling smile that made the sheriff inwardly shiver, and politely tipped his hat. 'I'll be riding on now.' He left as silently as he'd entered.

Sheriff Henson went to the window and looked out. The blond-haired man mounted an elegant, brown and white pinto with a white mane and long black tail, and rode off.

'Goddamn little shrimp,' Sheriff Henson muttered. 'He's lucky I didn't throw his puny ass in jail.'

3

As he rode out of town Blue warily checked every side-street and alley he passed in case any of the Dixons' relatives or friends were hiding there waiting to bushwhack him. He didn't expect any trouble because from what he'd heard about the twins, they had no family and few if any friends. But he kept looking anyway. In his profession one never knew when a vengeful relative of someone he'd shot was looking to kill him.

He was lucky this time. No ambush awaited him. Relieved, he rode on through the outskirts out into the desert scrubland.

As he rode, he reflected upon his past. It was something he always did after a killing. He didn't do it consciously. In fact, if someone had asked him why he did it, he would have been stuck for an answer. But then, a private man doesn't need answers and Egan Blue certainly was a private man.

He'd been a hired gun for almost two years now. It was a decision he'd made upon being told by a Dr. Arthur Grimes in Wichita that symptoms suggested Blue had a brain tumor and probably only a year or so to live. He added that though no surgeon as of yet had successfully removed a brain tumor, he'd heard of a doctor in Philadelphia named William Keens who was considering performing the procedure.

At first Blue had been bitter and resentful, blaming the Fates for singling him out and constantly asking himself: Why me?

But it wasn't his nature to whine or complain about misfortune. And he soon pulled himself together and decided that while he was alive he'd do something meaningful, something that would benefit the living. But, what?

Many ideas came to mind but none of them seemed important enough, so he dismissed them and went on thinking.

Eventually, after shooting a drunken gunman in Waco who was pistol-whipping a storekeeper for refusing to give him a free box of cartridges, Blue knew he'd found his calling: he'd spend the rest of his days ridding the west of men who deserved to die.

It was a good calling. But since he was only one man and towns were often more than a week's ride apart, he placed a discreet advertisement in newspapers wherever he went, offering his services for a price and expenses. The ad promised that he would *remove* any man who by threat of violence was forcing others to surrender their property or business. He would have liked to have been more specific, but he knew the law would arrest him if he used the word: kill.

Blue hadn't expected many responses. But to his surprise he soon had several clients, as he called them, and from then on he had never run out of deserving targets. More importantly, he'd already survived a year longer than the doctor had told him and was presently living on what he called: Borrowed Time . . .

4

Now, with the vast desert spread out before him, Blue urged the pinto into an easy, steady lope. The pinto was like the man who rode him: small, quiet and unassuming yet capable of unexpected feats. Five years ago Blue had rescued it from desert quicksand. From then on the pinto, whose whip-scarred brown-and-white coat showed it had been abused, had obeyed him. But it did so with an attitude that made it quite clear that it was willing to be obedient but not subservient.

Blue respected the stallion for that and treated it as an equal. He didn't know who had previously owned the pinto and even if he had, wouldn't have returned it for fear it would receive more whippings. He didn't name it, either, believing that he didn't have the right. Also, naming it would have suggested it was a pet and the horse was anything but.

If the pinto felt cheated for having no name, it never showed it. It did whatever it was asked without complaint or resistance and, in return, Blue never mistreated it. It was a harmonious relationship and gradually an inseparable bond developed between them.

As Blue rode across the flat, sun-baked scrubland that was barren save for patches of flowering cacti, he could feel all the tension draining out of his body. It felt good to relax. Due to constant headaches that lately had gotten worse, it was a luxury he seldom enjoyed and he gratefully thanked the Fates for protecting him against the Dixon brothers.

Getting shot wasn't something he dwelled upon. He knew he could slap leather faster than most, and, more importantly, had no fear of dying. It was an attitude that intimidated his targets, putting them at a disadvantage when he braced them. Admittedly, the possibility of having a terminal brain tumor made it easier for him to accept death, but that wasn't the only reason. As a young man on the prod, Blue had learned the same philosophy from an outlaw he'd befriended, the legendary Gabriel Moonlight.

'Never run scared,' Gabe had told him. 'We're all going to die sooner or later, and no amount of fear or running can change that. But until that day comes, *amigo,* face your fate head-on and more often than not, you'll come out on top.'

Remembering Gabe's words made Blue smile grimly. As a rebellious orphan who'd run away from countless foster homes, he'd grown up with a chip on his shoulder, never caring about anyone but himself and his own enjoyment. Like a carefree grasshopper, he'd jumped from one place or situation to another. Guiltless and often penniless, he'd supported himself by robbing stagecoaches and small-town banks all over Texas. His face soon appeared on Wanted posters with a 500-dollar price on his head. That was a fortune to some, and everywhere Blue went he was pursued by bounty hunters and lawmen looking to claim the reward. He could only gun down so many of them, and finally he was forced to flee across the border into the wastelands of New Mexico.

It was there, in a saloon in Santa Rosa that he'd met Gabriel Moonlight. With him was a small, handsome, smartly-dressed gunman named Latigo Rawlins who was faster on the draw than anyone, including Blue. He was also a born killer, who sadistically enjoyed gunning down anyone who annoyed him. At Gabe's advice, Blue stayed clear of Latigo. But finally he couldn't stand the senseless killing any longer and headed for Kansas.

There, his luck deserted him. While targeting a bank in Abilene, he'd had one of his seizures and collapsed on the sidewalk, attracting the attention of the local sheriff. Recognizing Blue from a Wanted poster, he'd arrested him and brought him before a bored Circuit Court judge who while reading his newspaper sentenced Blue to ten years. When Blue demanded a lawyer, the judge increased his sentence to twenty years, banged his gavel and went on reading.

Being imprisoned had driven Blue almost insane. Unable to stand being caged in a cramped cell, he volunteered for work on a road gang. The guards only mocked him. He was too puny to swing a pick all day, they said. And when he persisted, the cell block commander agreed — but only if Blue could whip him in a fight. Blue accepted, even though he knew that the commander was a former bare-knuckle prizefighter, and was taken by guards to the basement. There, his chains were removed and he was pushed into a ring that was chalked on the floor.

Surrounded by jeering guards, Blue took his beating in grim silence. He was no boxer and his opponent outweighed him by ninety pounds. Blue got in a few solid punches, but mostly he absorbed blow after blow until he was pummeled into a bloody, swollen mess. But he'd still gone on fighting until a sudden mild seizure turned his legs to jelly and he collapsed to the floor. By now, the guards had stopped jeering and were begging him to quit. Blue stubbornly refused and went on taking brutal punishment until the commander wouldn't hit him anymore. Blue numbly got to his feet, eyes swollen shut, fists cocked, ready to fight an opponent he couldn't see.

The commander eyed Blue with new-found respect and ordered the guards to clean him up and return him to his cell. Though the fight was supposed to be a secret, there are no secrets in prison and word quickly leaked out. As a result, the other inmates cheered Blue as he limped past their cells.

For the rest of the day and all that

night he lay on his bunk, barely conscious. By now he'd earned the guards' respect and they spoon-fed him soup and put wet towels on his face to lessen the swelling.

By morning Blue could see and was strong enough to stand. Though stiff and very sore from the pummeling, he ignored a blinding headache and again asked to be put on the road gang. The guards tried to dissuade him but he insisted. This time the commander grudgingly gave in. But only on the condition that Blue be the water-boy, whose duty was to make sure the workers got enough water so they could work all day in the searing heat.

Day after day, Blue trudged between the two lines of chained, sweat-soaked convicts, ladling out water when they were thirsty, while at the same time watching the rifle-toting guards, looking for that moment when he wasn't watched and could slip away, unnoticed, into the dense woods that bordered both sides of the road.

Finally, after a year of confinement and monotonous duty as a water-boy, his patience paid off. One bitter wintry morning when a fog hid the woods, a lifer named Belasco settled a grudge by burying his pick in the back of the convict in front of him. The man screamed and fell to his knees. His weight dragged down the convicts chained ahead of him, causing instant commotion.

Belasco pounced on his victim, wrapped the chain around his neck and choked him.

The guards furiously clubbed Belasco with their rifle butts. But he wasn't easy to subdue and before he could be beaten to the ground, he'd broken his victim's neck. Then, laughing insanely, he attacked the guards. Alarmed, they shot him and kept on shooting him until Belasco finally collapsed, dragging several other convicts down with him.

During the commotion, Blue saw his chance and sprinted for the woods. He reached the trees unnoticed and disappeared into the fog.

Despite an extensive manhunt, he was never caught or incarcerated again.

5

It was high noon and the broiling New Mexico sun was unbearable. Undulating heat waves distorted the distant horizon until it resembled a yellow ocean.

Blue reined in the weary pinto, shaded his squinted eyes and gazed about him. All he could see was sand and more sand. About to ride on, he spotted a small rocky outcrop in the distance. Grateful for even the slightest patch of shade, Blue nudged the pinto toward it. The horse welcomed the shade as much as the man and broke into a flagging gallop.

On reaching the rocks, Blue dismounted and loosened the girth strap to give the pinto a much-needed breather. He then removed the cap of his canteen and let a small amount of water trickle down his parched throat.

The water was warm and tasted coppery, but it was still refreshing and Blue had difficulty resisting the urge to drink more. Instead, he poured a little on his kerchief and wiped away the salt caked around the pinto's mouth. He then squeezed the water out of the kerchief into his cupped hand and fed it to the stallion, which greedily lapped it up.

'I know it ain't much,' Blue admitted, 'but I got to save what's left in case the next water hole is dried up.'

The pinto snorted, as if understanding and moved up against the rocks where the shade was coolest. Blue untied his bedroll and spread it out near the sweat-caked stallion. He needed to relieve himself, but since he was so dehydrated he decided not to let even the smallest amount of water escape from his system.

Once stretched out on his blanket, Blue rolled a smoke, flared a match on his jeans and lit up. He inhaled deeply. The taste of tobacco as the smoke hit his lungs not only was intoxicating, but helped deaden his headache. Blue closed his dry, sweat-crusted eyes and silently thanked the gods for inventing smoking.

While he smoked, he thought about the letter in his pocket. He didn't need to read it; he'd memorized every word. It was from the mayor of San Dimas. In a literate hand that indicated he was educated, Mayor Colton explained that Blue's services were needed right away as the homesteaders and smaller ranches were being terrorized by gunmen. Masked, they only came at night, burning crops and homes and stealing livestock and threatening to kill the owners if they didn't sell out and move away. Fearful for their lives, many homesteaders had already left, selling their land for a pittance to a lawyer who claimed his firm represented a wealthy, out-of-town client. If Blue agreed to drive off the gunmen and stop all future death threats, the mayor and the Town Council would pay his fee and his expenses for as long as it took him to achieve his goal.

Blue had wired Mayor Colton back, promising to be in San Dimas within five days.

Tomorrow was the fifth day and as Blue crushed out his smoke and rolled up his blanket, he wondered how many gunmen he'd have to kill before the unnamed client would throw in the towel.

Going to the pinto, which was dozing on its feet, Blue tied his bedroll behind the saddle and tightened the cinch. Unlike many horses that slyly took a deep breath and held it, enlarging their girth as the strap was fastened under its belly, the pinto was always cooperative. Never once in all the years he'd saddled the stallion had Blue needed to knee it in the belly to force it to exhale so that the tightness of the cinch was accurate.

Now was no exception. Satisfied, Blue grasped the reins, stepped up into the saddle and nudged the pinto forward. Still drowsy, the honest little horse was reluctant to leave the shade and walked alongside the row of rocks that were as tall as most trees.

Blue was equally drowsy. Unsure whether it was because of the intense heat or just a another of his recurring symptoms, he toyed with the idea of staying in the shade until the sun went down and then traveling at night. It was tempting. But his integrity wouldn't let him rest any longer. It reminded him that he'd promised Mayor Colton that he'd be in San Dimas within five days. It also reminded him that a man was only as good as his word. And intense as the heat was, Blue kept going.

As he rode past the last rock he heard a low growl. It was a growl he'd heard before during his travels and as he looked up in alarm, a cougar leaped off the rocks at him.

Blue quickly grabbed for his six-gun. But the sleek tawny cat was quicker. It hit him before the revolver cleared leather, knocking him from the saddle. He landed hard, breath slammed out of him, helpless against the snarling cougar's attack.

Blue rolled over on his side and huddled up in an effort to protect his face, throat and belly. But that left the rest of him vulnerable. He felt the big cat's claws raking across his shoulders while its fangs sank into the back of his neck, the pain making Blue scream.

Mingled in with his scream was another louder scream that came from the pinto. Though terrified, it charged the mountain lion, rearing up and stomping the big cat with its hooves. Fearing for its life the cougar released its hold on Blue's neck, whirled and growled at the enraged stallion. But the pinto wouldn't stop. Again and again it reared up, hooves flailing, hammering the cat until it was forced to back away. But the cougar was hungry and once out of range of the pinto's hooves, it stopped and turned around, ears flattened, fangs bared, snarling as it crouched ready to spring at the horse.

Meanwhile Blue, bleeding from wounds

on his neck and back, managed to sit up and draw his gun. Holding it with both hands, he aimed it at the cougar and kept squeezing the trigger until the gun was empty. By then the bullet-riddled cat lay bleeding on its side, legs twitching, dying.

6

Barely conscious, Blue watched as the cougar gave a final shudder and died. He then turned to the pinto which stood, eyes aflame, nostrils flared, trembling before him.

Blue shook his head at it. 'I don't know whether to thank you, or curse you for saving my life,' he said.

The pinto snorted and pawed at the dirt.

'Reckon for now I'll thank you,' Blue said. He paused, waiting for the world around him to stop spinning, and tried to stand up. It was useless. His legs buckled the instant he put his weight on them.

'Not good,' he muttered. 'Not good at all.' He tried again with the same result — only this time he blacked out. When he came around and could see again, he sat there for a few minutes in the broiling sun, wondering what to do next. Nothing came to him and he was forced to accept the fact that possibly — even probably he was going to die out here.

The pinto had other ideas. Sensing something was wrong, it came and stood beside Blue so that one of the stirrups dangled inches from his face.

It took Blue a few moments to realize what the pinto was trying to tell him. But once he did he reached up, grabbed the stirrup and tried to pull himself to his feet. But he was too weak from loss of blood and he collapsed again. Desperate, he suddenly had an idea. With great effort, he slipped his hand and wrist through the stirrup. When the stirrup reached up to his elbow, he bent his arm downward, hooking it in position. He then one-handedly unbuckled his belt and after much struggling, managed to pull it loose. Dizzy from the effort, he sat still for a spell, blood misting before his eyes. Eventually he managed to blink it away, enabling him to see more clearly. He quickly wrapped the belt around his arm and the stirrup, locking them together. The effort exhausted him and he blacked out again.

When he came around, the pinto was still standing patiently beside him.

'Okay,' he told it. 'Now it's up to you whether I live or die.'

The pinto snorted and tossed its head, sweat spraying everywhere.

Some of it splashed on Blue's face. It was the last thing he remembered.

7

When he regained consciousness his arm was still tied to the stirrup and he had an ungodly thirst. He noticed the sun was no longer directly overhead and he was covered in dirt and blood. He looked around and realized he could no longer see the rocks. Guessing that the pinto had dragged him here — wherever 'here' was — Blue tucked his legs under him and tried to get to his knees, hoping he could drag himself up high enough to reach the canteen hanging from his saddle horn.

'Easy . . . easy,' a voice said behind him. 'You've lost too much blood already.'

Startled, Blue turned and saw a man crouched nearby. He was a big man who despite the heat wore a black hat pulled down low, a black western-styled suit and a string tie with a turquoise clasp. Holstered on his hips were two fancy ivory-gripped, nickel-plated Colt .45s. He studied Blue, curious and concerned, one hand holding the reins of a magnificent dappled gray with a long white mane and flowing white tail that reached almost to the ground.

'W-Who're you?' Blue croaked, not recognizing his own voice.

'Name's Hunt Logan,' the man replied. He stood up, tall, lean and big-shouldered, as handsome as any man Blue had ever seen. He also exuded a boyish charm that made it hard to judge his age — though he couldn't have been more than thirty. But it was easy to see why he was so good-looking. His hair was black and roguishly curly, his gray eyes full of impudent charm, and below his dimpled cheeks was a smile that could have melted stone. 'Lucky for you I was out looking for strays,' he said, handing Blue his canteen. 'Another mile or two and you wouldn't have been worth saving.'

Blue eagerly drank some water and then forced himself to hand the canteen back to Logan. 'I'd appreciate it, mister, if you'd give my horse some.'

'Already done that,' Logan said. 'Figured since you owed him your life, the least he deserved was to drink first.'

'Amen,' said Blue. He looked fondly at the pinto. 'That's the second time he's saved my life. But for him, I'd be chewing meat for a cougar that jumped me.'

'I wondered what scratched you up like that,' Logan said. 'Figured it was either a cougar or an ocelot that'd wandered up from Chihuahua. But listen, enough talk for now. We got to get you to Doc Ahearn, so he can cleanse those wounds and stitch you up 'fore you lose any more blood.' Rising, he untied the belt holding Blue's arm to the stirrup and slipped his hands under Blue's armpits. 'This may hurt some, mister . . .'

'Don't worry about that,' Blue said, grimacing as Logan stood him upright and then heaved him onto the saddle. 'I'm just glad . . . ' He broke off as a wave of excruciating pain hit him. Dizzy and nauseated, he fought not to pass out. He lost the battle and felt himself slide into silent, inky darkness.

8

The two-mile ride to San Dimas was a painful hazy blur to Blue. He had a violent headache and kept drifting in and out of consciousness. He would have fallen from the saddle many times if Logan, who was riding alongside him, hadn't grabbed his arm and steadied him until Blue regained control of himself.

The trail that led to the little town was relatively recent. As of yet no great cattle herds had been driven along it, and because San Dimas was not considered a stepping stone to an already established town or city there weren't even a lot of wagon-wheel ruts.

But according to the ever-optimistic local newspaper, *The Desert Sun*, things were changing. San Dimas, the editor claimed, due to recent gold and silver strikes in the surrounding hills, would soon rival or surpass its larger, more populated neighbors. Naturally, the editor never mentioned the rash of night raids by masked gunmen that was forcing the frightened homesteaders to sell their land and move away. He knew that if newcomers caught wind of these deadly attacks they would bypass San Dimas and settle elsewhere and the town would continue to have what he called an 'identity crisis!'

When Blue and Logan rode into town, curious passersby stopped and stared at them. They recognized Logan, but wondered who the badly bleeding stranger was and how he had managed to stay alive in his condition.

Logan smiled and waved at everyone they passed. He was well-liked in San Dimas and was about to increase his popularity by marrying Hillary Darby, the adopted daughter of the late Owen Darby, the recently-deceased owner of the Sundown Ranch. Hilly, as she was called, was not only popular but refreshingly pretty, and everybody was eager to greet the beautiful babies they expected the attractive couple to have.

'We're almost there,' Logan told Blue as they reached the center of town. 'The doc's office is just ahead.'

Blue didn't respond. Barely conscious, he felt his life slipping away and was helpless to stop it. Worse; he wasn't sure if he wanted to.

Shortly, Logan reined up outside McVicar's Livery Stable, dismounted and gently helped Blue down from the pinto. Next door was a small, nondescript wood-frame building with two entrances. Nailed to the posts supporting the overhanging roof were two shingles. One read: Lewis R. Ahearn, MD, the other: L. Horace Demarest, mortician.

'Don't worry about the signs,' Logan said as he helped Blue to the doctor's office. 'One has no bearing on the other. It just so happens that Horace and the doc are married to sisters and figured sharing space wouldn't only save money but would keep everything in the family.'

Before they got to the door it swung open and a short, balding, big-bellied man of sixty hurried out to help them.

'Mother of God,' he breathed as he saw Blue's blood-soaked clothing. 'What the hell happened to this man, Hunt?'

'Cougar got him, doc. Reckon he'd be dead by now but for his horse.'

'Help me get him inside,' Dr. Ahearn said, 'and then tend to that poor animal. It looks like it's lost almost as much blood as this man.'

'That's the rub,' Logan said. 'The horse don't have a scratch on him. All that blood belongs to him.' He nodded at Blue.

Dr. Ahearn looked even more concerned, but didn't say anything. Together, they carried Blue into the small spartanly-clean office and put him on the examination table. There, the doctor gently peeled off Blue's clothing and with Logan's help managed to cover his naked, blood-streaked body with a smock.

'Okay, okay,' Dr. Ahearn said. 'You've

done all you can, Hunt. Now, get out of here and let me stop the bleeding so Langdon can clean him up and get his grave dug.'

'Dammit, doc,' Logan grumbled. 'Do you have to be so pessimistic? This fella's gone through enough hell without you burying him 'fore his time.'

Mercifully, Blue didn't hear the doctor or Logan.

He'd already passed out.

9

After leaving the doctor's office, Logan turned the pinto over to the livery stable owner, Duncan McVicar. A small, sour-faced Scotsman in his fifties, whose accent got thicker after he'd had a few whiskies, he openly hated horses and had only taken over his late father's business because it was prospering.

'Whoa,' he said as Logan started to mount the gray. 'Where, pray tell, do ye think you're going?'

'To meet Hilly. I promised to help her pick out — '

'Nae, nae, laddie. You'll not be going anywhere — least, not till we settle who's going to pay for stalling and graining this brute should its owner die.'

'Who says he's going to die, you penny-pinching old highlander?'

'Why you did, laddie.'

'Like hell I did! All I said was, the man had been chewed up by a cougar and had lost a lot of blood.'

'Same thing, would ye nae say? Anyway, leave us not quibble, laddie. Money is money and someone has to pay me. I'm nae running a charity home here, ye know.'

'Calm down,' Logan soothed. 'No need to blow wind up your kilt. If the man dies, I'll make sure you get paid, Scotty — even if I have to pay you myself. Fair enough?'

'Aye,' McVicar said. 'But should he linger on for more than a few days, I'll be expecting ye to help with the expenses. Dinna think I won't.'

'That's not something either of us has to worry about,' Logan said. 'This fella will be lucky if he lasts till sundown.' He swung up into the saddle and rode out of the stable, leaving the pinto in the hands of the irascible, money-grubbing Scotsman.

* * *

53

Next door in the doctor's office Blue was still unconscious. It was just as well. Dr. Ahearn had been as gentle as he could while tending to all the scratches and bites, but he knew how excruciating the pain must be and worked as fast as he could in an effort to finish all the stitching before his patient came around.

His biggest problem had been the four deep puncture wounds on the back of Blue's neck. The cougar's fangs had pierced the flesh so deeply, Dr. Ahearn was forced to use his scalpel to cut away the surrounding flesh in order to properly cleanse the wounds, and was now hurriedly trying to sew them closed before Blue awoke.

A grimaced, clinched-teeth groan from his patient told the doctor he had lost the race.

'Hang in there, son,' he told Blue. 'I'm almost finished.'

Blue gave a weak nod to show he'd heard, but kept his eyes closed. His cracked, sunburned lips worked with great effort as they tried to form words. But the sound that came out of them was barely human and Dr. Ahearn immediately hushed him, saying softly: 'No more talking, please. Just concentrate all your strength on staying alive. It's your only priority right now.' Even as he spoke, he knew that his patient's chances of surviving without a blood transfusion were almost nil, but remembering Logan's chiding remark about pessimism, kept his opinion to himself.

The tinkling of the tiny bell above the door told him he had another patient. He started to call out that he was busy and wouldn't be out for a while — when there were two polite knocks on the door of the examination room.

'I'm busy right now, Hilly,' he said, recognizing her double knock. 'Is it important?'

'No, I just wanted to ask you something and then I'll scoot.'

'All right, stick your head in.'

The door opened and Hilly entered. She was a naturally pretty young woman with fine features, expressive hazel eyes and a warm smile whose sun-bronzed skin contrasted sharply against her flaxen hair.

'I don't mean to bother you, doc, but have you seen Hunt lately? He was supposed to meet me at the baker's to help pick out our wedding cake and — '

'He was here a little while ago,' Dr. Ahearn interrupted. He paused and dabbed the sweat from his face before adding: 'He brought this patient in, in fact.'

'Who is he?' Hilly asked, coming closer.

Dr. Ahearn shrugged and went on stitching. 'Just someone Hunt found in the desert. Said a cougar attacked him. Poor fella's been unconscious most of the time, so I've no idea where he's from or anything else about him. Did you check next door?' he added. 'Hunt agreed to stable this man's horse till we knew if he was going to make it or not.'

'Thanks, doc.' Hill turned to leave and then, as if drawn to Blue, looked curiously at him, asking: 'Think he will?'

'What — make it?' Dr. Ahearn shrugged doubtfully. 'It'll be a miracle if he does. He's lost buckets of blood and unfortunately I've been so busy making sure he doesn't lose any more to find out what type it is, so even if I had blood, which I don't, I couldn't — '

'He can have some of mine,' Hilly offered.

'That's very kind of you, dear, but — '

'I know, I know, my blood might not match his. But so what? You said he's going to die soon anyway, so what difference does it make how? You can't be choosy when you need a miracle, right? And I'm as close to a miracle as he's going to get. I mean, if Hunt had met me as promised, I wouldn't even be here, so — '

Dr. Ahearn, who'd been listening but at the same time calculating the odds of Hilly and Blue having the same type blood, said suddenly: 'You're right! This is no time for indecision. We must act! Roll up your sleeve, young lady, and let's hope for a miracle.'

10

The transfusion was a success.

Shortly after Blue had received blood from Hilly, his feeble pulse became stronger and he gradually regained some color in his pale, drawn face. His eyelids, motionless up till now, started fluttering and when Dr. Ahearn asked Blue if he could hear him, he seemed to struggle within himself for a few moments and then opened his eyes, wide.

'Well, now, that's more like it,' said Dr. Ahearn, smiling. 'Welcome back, soldier!'

Blue blinked a few times, as if trying to focus, and then weakly moved his lips. His voice was too faint to hear at first. But when Dr. Ahearn leaned over and put his ear against Blue's mouth, he heard enough to make him smile.

Straightening up, he said to Hilly:

'Wanted to know if I was finished sewing him up.'

'That's a good sign?'

'The best. Means he's coherent.' He paused and shook his head in amazement. 'I'm not exactly what you'd call a religious man, Hilly, but, dammit, his recovery from death's door is — well, close enough to a miracle to make a believer out of me.'

'Maybe he was put here for a purpose? You know, to invent a cure for smallpox or — or discover a new trail to Oregon or — '

'Get rid of flies or mosquitoes,' Dr. Ahearn joked as he slapped an insect from his neck.

'Don't laugh,' Hilly chided. 'Stranger things have happened, as Owen used to say.'

'I thought his pet phrase was' — Dr. Ahearn struck a presidential pose and mimicked Owen's voice — 'Lewis, my good man, there's a whole lot going in this universe that we aren't aware of.'

Hilly, though drained, managed a

tiny laugh. 'My God, doc, that's perfect. If I'd had my eyes shut I would've sworn it was Owen.'

Dr. Ahearn chuckled. ''Tween helping him run for mayor twice and Wednesday night poker games, I've had lots of practice. Speaking of poker,' he added, 'did you know your stepdad used to cheat?'

'Sadly yes,' she replied, amused. 'And it didn't stop at poker. I've lost count of the times I've caught him cheating at solitaire.'

'Bet he denied it.'

'With all his might,' Hilly began, then stopped as a low groan came from Blue.

Both of them moved close to the examination table where Blue was stirring, each slight shift of position making him grunt painfully.

Hilly looked concerned. 'Isn't there something you can do to relieve his pain?'

Dr. Ahearn shook his head. ''Fraid I've done all I can, dear.'

61

'I feel so helpless.'

'Why? You've already saved his life. What more can anyone expect?'

'I don't know. It's just so . . . frustrating.' She sighed and wearily closed her eyes.

'You'd better go lie down for a spell, young lady.'

'No, no, I'm all right. I — '

'Don't argue with your doctor.' He thumbed at the door to an inner office. 'There's a couch in there. Help yourself to it for as long as like.'

'Thanks, maybe I will . . . ' Hilly yawned, gave another weary sigh and gazed at Blue. 'Do me a favor, doc?'

'Of course.'

'If I'm asleep when he's ready to leave, wake me up, will you? I'd like to meet him.'

'Sure.'

'Promise?'

'Promise. Now . . . be a good girl and go rest.'

He waited until Hilly had entered the inner office and closed the door then turned back to Blue, who was now awake and trying to shake off the cobwebs.

'Who was that?' Blue asked hoarsely.

Dr. Ahearn smiled. 'Oh-h . . . just your average run-of-the-mill miracle worker.'

11

Once Blue was finally patched up Dr. Ahearn suggested that he get a room at the Hotel Palomar and rest there till the next morning.

Blue, still groggy, grudgingly agreed and looked around. 'Where're my clothes?'

'I gave them to the Chinaman.'

'You had 'em washed?'

'I had no choice. They were so caked with blood, it was either burn them or wash them. If you're short on money, son, I'll put it on my bill and you can pay me back later.'

'I ain't short on money,' Blue said, adding: 'Any idea how long it's going to take?'

Dr. Ahearn looked at the clock on the wall, calculated how long it had been since he gave Blue's clothes to the Chinaman and said: 'Exactly seven more minutes. Come to think of it,' he continued, 'that should work out perfectly.'

'Meaning?'

'There's someone who made me promise not to let you leave without meeting her.'

'Her?' Blue frowned, momentarily puzzled. 'That's impossible, doc. I don't know any women here.'

'You know this one. And she surely knows you.' Before Blue could ask any more questions, Dr. Ahearn went to the inner office door and knocked. 'Hilly,' he called out. 'Hilly, wake up. Mr. Blue's getting ready to leave.'

'Be right there,' she replied sleepily.

Blue again looked puzzled. 'Hilly?' he said, trying to place the name. 'Doc, I swear I don't know anyone called — ' He broke off as the inner door opened and Hilly appeared.

'Hello,' she said, approaching Blue. 'Glad to see you're up and around.'

Blue smiled hesitantly, still trying to place Hilly.

'Perhaps I should introduce myself,' she said, offering him her hand. 'I'm Hillary Darby. But everyone calls me Hilly.'

Blue nodded politely and shook hands. 'I go by Egan Blue.'

'Nice meeting you again, Egan Blue.'

'Again?' Blue looked questioningly at her. 'I'm sorry, miss, but you must have me mixed up with someone else.'

Hillary turned to Dr. Ahearn. 'Guess you haven't told him yet?'

'Uh-uh. Figured that was your right.'

'Told me what?' Blue interrupted. 'Will someone tell me what's going on?'

Dr. Ahearn said: 'Remember that miracle worker I told you about? Well, you're looking at her.'

'Aw, doc,' Hilly said. 'Don't exaggerate. It's not like I did anything special.' To Blue she added: 'You needed blood. I happened to be here. I gave you some. That's it. Plain and simple.'

'That was mighty kind of you, miss. I surely appreciate it.'

'You should,' Dr. Ahearn said. 'She

66

saved your life, soldier. I'd say that was special, wouldn't you?'

'I would indeed,' Blue said, at the same time wondering if his maker was maliciously keeping him alive so he could suffer. 'I wish there was something I could do to really express my thanks, Miss — '

'Hilly,' she reminded. 'And as for doing something, you've already done it. You're alive. That's more than enough thanks for me.' Before Blue could respond, she pecked Dr. Ahearn on the cheek and hurried out.

Blue sat up, feeling like he'd been injected with a breath of fresh air.

Dr. Ahearn went to the window and gazed out. Lost in thought, he watched Hilly ride away, his expression revealing just how much she meant to him.

'You know,' he said after a pause, 'it's hard to believe that twenty-odd years have passed since I brought that little girl into the world . . . ' He turned to Blue, his voice still savoring the past as he added: 'She was three weeks premature and so tiny I was afraid she might not make it. But I underestimated her will to live.' Memories made him smile. 'She had this almost transparent skin that looked blue because the blood vessels were visible. There were wisps of yellow hair sticking to her forehead and her little face was all pinched up like a dried fig. As for her hands and feet, I swear they were no bigger than grapes. And her fingers and toes, my God, they were so tiny and yet perfectly formed. Believe me, Mr. Blue, I've delivered my fair share of babies over the years and I can truthfully say, none gave me more pleasure than Hilly.'

Blue, caught up in the doctor's euphoria, compared the doctor's life to his own and found his lacking. 'Must be quite a thrill, doc, knowing you've given life to something.'

'I don't give life, soldier. I leave that to a higher power. I'm just the instrument the Good Lord uses to deliver His flock.'

Blue, amused by the irony, thought: And I'm the instrument He uses to cull His flock.

Just then the little bell above the door in the outer office tinkled as someone entered.

'Reckon that's the Chinaman,' Dr. Ahearn said. He looked at the clock on the wall. 'Seven minutes exactly. One hour on the nose. I swear you could set your watch by him.'

12

After leaving Dr. Ahearn's office, Blue limped to the livery stable and made sure the pinto was stalled and fed. He was still weak and even talking was an effort. McVicar noticed this and took advantage of him, demanding that he pay one dollar a day — in advance! Blue, too exhausted to argue, grudgingly coughed up the money and left.

Outside, a wave of dizziness hit him and he felt the strength leaving his left leg. It was another of the many symptoms caused by the brain tumor and he stood there, blinking in the late-afternoon sun, trying to focus on the pedestrians, riders and wagons passing before him. It took several minutes, but when he could see clearly he looked around for the Hotel Palomar, which he vaguely remembered Dr. Ahearn recommending.

'Mister?' a voice said politely. ''Scuse me for asking, but are you lost?'

Blue turned and saw a girl standing before him. No more than twelve, she wore an old straw hat with a wide brim to protect her almost luminous pink-white skin from the sun and ragged hand-me-down bib-coveralls that were too big for her scrawny body. Her pale bare feet were dirty and callused from never knowing shoes and the all-white pigtail hanging from under her hat reached to her waist. But unusual as those things were, it was her pinkish eyes that caught Blue's attention. Below eyebrows and lashes so fair they were almost invisible, they seemed to have no pupils and looked up at him like large blood moons. Though he'd once seen an albino in a traveling freak show, at the time he'd been standing at the back of a large crowd and was too far away to appreciate the man's uniqueness. But this young girl was right before him, close enough to touch, and Blue found the experience unnerving.

'W-What did you say?' he asked.

'Are you lost?' she repeated. 'I mean, it's none of my business, mister, but I've never seen you in town afore and by the way you kept looking 'round, I figured — '

Blue stopped her. 'The Hotel Palomar?' he said. 'Can — you tell me where it is?'

'Sure, mister. But . . . ' she eyed him dubiously, 'it's a far piece down the street and — '

'Never mind how far it is. Just point the way, missy — '

'Maddy. My name's Maddy. Maddy Philo.'

'Maddy — and I'll get to it.'

She gave him another dubious look. Then with a shrug that suggested grownups were really the children of the world, she said, 'Better follow me, mister,' and started away.

Blue followed her but after a few wobbly steps, halted and said: 'Whoa, not so fast.'

The girl stopped and waited until he

caught up. Then grasping his hand and assuming the role of a mother taking her child to school, she led him along the hot dusty street.

It was no more than a hundred yards to the Hotel Palomar, but by the time Bluc reached the entrance he was beyond exhausted.

'You going to be all right, mister?'

Blue nodded, unconvincingly, and reached into his pocket. 'Here . . . take this.' He offered her all the change he had: three nickels.

She looked indignant. 'Keep it, mister. Money ain't why I helped you. That's a fact.'

'Never said it was. But since I wouldn't have made it without you, it's only fair and proper you get paid for helping me.'

Finding his logic acceptable, she tucked the nickels into her coveralls. 'In that case, c'mon,' she said, and grasping his hand led him into the hotel.

Behind the front desk stood a tall, stern-faced woman who thanks to loneliness, long hours in a ruthless climate and the loss of her husband to Blackwater fever looked older than her fifty-one years. But there was no quit in her. Behind wire-frame glasses her sad brown eyes spoke of grit and intelligence, and she carried herself with austere dignity.

She brightened as she saw Maddy and leaning her elbows on the desk, said: 'Well, well, what a pleasant surprise. What brings you to town, Sunshine?'

'It's my uncle, here,' Maddy said, indicating Blue. 'He wants a room.'

'Y-Your *uncle*?'

'Yeah. As you can see, he got all ate up by a mountain lion and needs to rest. That's a fact.'

'Yes, yes, obviously . . . ' Mrs. Strazinsky looked at Blue with a mixture of curiosity and wry amusement. 'Your uncle, eh?' she repeated.

Maddy nodded emphatically. 'Do you got a room, Mrs. Strazinsky?'

'I do indeed.' She turned the register

toward Blue and offered him a pen. 'If you'll sign here, please, Mr . . . uh — ?'

'Blue, ma'am. Egan Blue.'

Mrs. Strazinksy watched him sign and then dried his signature with blotting paper.

'Strange,' she said to Maddy, 'I've known you and your Uncle John for years and I never even knew you had another uncle.'

'That's 'cause he's been away,' Maddy said quickly. 'Abilene, wasn't it, uncle?'

'Fort Worth.'

'Oh, that's right. I forgot.'

'And how did you like Fort Worth, Mr. Blue?' Mrs. Strazinksy asked.

'I prefer it here, ma'am.'

'Spoken like a true diplomat, Mr. Blue. But I can't fault you. I'm from Kansas City and I prefer it here myself. By the way, sir, will you be staying more than one night?'

'No, ma'am. I'll be gone come sunup.'

'Very well.'

'One other thing,' Blue said. 'My saddlebags and saddle are at the livery stable.'

'Don't worry, I'll have the porter bring them to you.' She made a notation in the register before adding: 'Now, about the room rate. Because you're Maddy's uncle — '

Blue, deciding the charade had lasted long enough, said: 'Ma'am, I'm not — '

'*And* a patient of Dr. Ahearn's,' she continued, signaling with her eyes that she was just playing along, 'I'll be happy to give you our special rate of three dollars per.'

'That's mighty generous of you.'

'Don't forget my commission,' Maddy whispered to Mrs. Strazinksy. 'Mr. Doyle's got some new hard candy in and I want to buy some 'fore it's all gone. That's a fact.'

'Of course.' She took two cents from the register and handed them to Maddy. 'Here you are. Now, why don't you go splurge while I show Mr. Blue to his room.'

Maddy, though anxious to leave, looked at Blue and hesitated.

'It's okay,' he assured her. 'I can handle things from here on.'

'You sure, uncle?'

'Positive.'

'All right. But if you need any-thing — '

'I'll let you know,' he promised.

'How? You don't know where I live.'

'I do,' Mrs. Strazinksy reminded. 'And I'll be happy to pass along any messages he has. Now, go buy that candy. Hurry.'

Maddy grinned, said, 'Bye, uncle,' to Blue and ran out.

'That's one sweet child,' Mrs. Strazinsky said, leading Blue to the stairs.

'Seems like.'

'No, no, take my word for it. Maddy has no dark side hiding inside her, itching to get out. She's one of those rare human beings who are what we think they are. I've known her since she was a toddler and I assure you, she doesn't have an evil thought in her entire body. Which in itself is remarkable enough. But when you consider what the poor child's been through, all the staring and insults she's had to endure, all the hateful teasing by other kids, and, worst of all, the death of her folks at the hands of Comanches — well, it's nothing short of amazing. But of course,' she added wryly, 'being her 'uncle', you already know that.'

'Don't be too hard on her for that, ma'am. She was just trying to get me a cheap rate.'

'Oh, I know that, Mr. Blue. Poor Maddy, she can't even tell a white lie without it being obvious.'

'Hard to hate her for that,' Blue said.

'What isn't obvious, though,' Mrs. Strazinsky continued as if he hadn't spoken, 'at least, not until you really get to know Maddy, is the fact that she always has a deeper motive for doing something. She may not mention it, but it's there all right, just below the surface, ready to pop up at a moment's notice. Like the tip of an iceberg, so to speak.'

They'd reached the top of the stairs and Blue paused, faintly dizzy from the climb.

'Seems like Maddy's more complicated than I figured, ma'am.'

'She is, Mr. Blue. Despite her sweet innocence, she's very complicated. And for good reason, I might add. My God, the way life's treated her is so appalling it would put one of Mr. Shakespeare's tragedies to shame.' Handing him his key, she pointed down the hallway of closed doors, 'Two-eleven is at the very end, on the left,' and then hurried off, leaving Blue full of unanswered questions.

13

He'd not been in his room very long when the hotel porter arrived with his saddle, saddlebags and bedroll. Blue left the saddle by the door and set the other things on the bed. He then made sure the door was locked before returning to the bed and examining the contents of his saddlebags.

Nothing was missing. Neither had anyone gone through his gear. He knew that by the fact that his skinning knife still lay on top of his tobacco pouch, underwear and socks. But just to be sure, he unfolded his bedroll and patted one end of the heavy wool blanket.

The last three inches were folded over and sewn together. Blue cut the stitching with his Bowie and upended the blanket. A mix of 20-dollar gold pieces and 20-dollar bank notes spilled out onto the mattress. Blue counted the money and looked relieved when it came to eight thousand, six hundred dollars! It was the total amount of money that he'd charged clients to kill their targets, minus his living expenses. And all the time he was saving, he kept hoping that he'd cheat death long enough to be able to restore the family mansion in Atlanta which General Sherman's troops had torched during their triumphant march through Georgia.

It was a dream he'd had since childhood. The one constant in his life, it had sustained him, nurtured him and even kept him sane during his darkest moments. He'd also used it as additional justification for killing his targets. But despite its significance, lately he'd begun to doubt it would ever be fulfilled. Much as he hated to admit it, daily the dream seemed to be less and less important to him. He wasn't sure why, but sensed it was because the memory of that ungodly tragedy was so distant now, and growing more distant by the day that he found it difficult to keep the image fresh in his mind. Even more disturbing, as the image faded so did his rage and need for revenge.

A knock on the door interrupted his thoughts. Taking his gun from the holster he limped to the door, asking: 'Who is it?'

'Hunt Logan — the fella who found you in the desert and took you to Dr. Ahearn.'

'Hang on,' Blue said. Tucking the gun in his pants, he unlocked the door and looked gratefully at Logan. 'Come on in . . . '

'Thanks.'

'I can't recall if I thanked you for saving my life,' Blue said as Logan entered, 'but — '

'I ain't here for your thanks, *amigo*.'

'What, then?'

'My boss sent me to invite you out to the ranch.'

'Why?' Blue said, puzzled.

'She figures you'll be more comfortable there while you're healing.'

'Why would she care about my comfort?'

'I asked her the same question.'

'And?'

'Said she feels like she has a stake in your future, being that she shared her blood with you today.'

Blue looked enlightened. 'Miss Hilly's your boss?'

'Uh-huh. And my fiancée.' Logan grinned, all dimples and teeth. 'Don't look so confused. Hilly and me, we're about to tie the knot and I still ain't got her figured out.'

Blue felt a stab of disappointment on hearing that Hilly was engaged to be married and immediately wondered why. Even before he'd learned he had a brain tumor, the fact that he was wanted and always on the run had stopped him from allowing himself to have any feelings for women and those that showed interest in him, he pushed away. It made for a lonely life but he accepted it, as he accepted he had a tumor, and whenever his lust could no longer be ignored, he satisfied himself with the nearest whore.

Logan's boisterous laughter, as he joked about something he'd just said, jerked Blue out of his reverie.

'Like all women,' Logan continued, 'it's easier to go along with them than argue. 'Cause either way, you're going to end up doing what they want, so why fight it, I say.'

Blue didn't reply, but Logan took his silence to mean yes and laughed boisterously again. Anxious to get rid of him, Blue was about to say he wasn't interested in Hilly's offer, when Logan said:

'Look, 'fore you say no, let me throw in my two cents. As foreman of the Darby outfit, I know a good man when I see one. And you're aces. While I was bringing you out of the desert you showed the kind of grit most men wish for and never get, and I figure you'd be a real asset to have around. I got a good crew now and you'd only make it better.'

Blue frowned. 'This job offer — does it come from you or Hilly?'

'Me. Hilly always backs my play, but as foreman I do the hiring and the firing. I know you didn't ask for work, but — '

'Man can always use work,' Blue said.

'Then we're in accord,' Logan said happily. 'I'm looking to hire an extra hand and unless you think you couldn't work for me, Hilly's offer now makes even more sense.'

'How so?'

'The way I figure it, while you're getting your legs under you, you can see firsthand how I run things. Then you can draw your own conclusions and decide whether you want to throw in with us or not. The ranch is growing bigger by the day and so is our herd.'

'Which means you need a bigger crew?'

'Exactly.'

'Seems I'm in the right place at the right time, for once,' Blue said, thinking aloud.

'Yes and no. By that, I mean you wouldn't be just another hand.'

Blue's eyes hardened. 'You're hiring me for my gun, that it?'

Logan nodded. 'But not like you might think. Lately, the whole valley's been plagued by rustlers — us included. And from what I've heard about you — from men who've run cattle from here to Texas — you could be the answer to our problem.'

Blue didn't agree but he didn't disagree either.

Encouraged, Logan continued. 'So, here's my proposition: Accept Hilly's hospitality, and while you're healing, nose around, size things up, see if you think we're the kind of outfit you could work for. Oh, and, hopefully, put an end to the rustling.'

Blue thought a moment and then nodded. 'All right. But I can't ride out tonight. Right now I hurt too bad to even think about sitting on a horse.'

'I figured that might be the case,' Logan said. 'That's why I brought the buggy. Not the softest ride, maybe, but better than a horse.'

'Seem like you've thought of everything.'

'I try.'

'Lot of folks try,' Blue said, 'you seem to succeed.'

'Hope you're not going to hold that against me?'

Blue shrugged noncommittally. 'Talking of horses,' he said, 'what about mine?'

'Tomorrow I'll have one of my men ride in and pick him up for you. I stabled him at McVicar's, so he'll be fine for tonight.'

'That's another thing I got to thank you for.'

'You'd do the same for me, wouldn't you?' Before Blue could more than nod, Logan added: 'Anything else you need taken care of?'

'Not off the top of my head.'

'Then what's your answer?'

Mind on Hilly, Blue said: 'I accept.' Then as Logan beamed: 'But I'm not promising anything, you understand? If after I've looked around I feel like it's not a good fit, I'll ride on as soon as I'm healed. Fair enough?'

Logan grinned and stuck out a big meaty hand. 'More than fair, *amigo*.'

14

As they rode in the buggy across the valley in the waning dusk, Blue wincing at every jolting bump, he asked himself a question that had been gnawing at him ever since he'd accepted Logan's offer: did his unusual interest in Hilly have anything to do with why he'd finally agreed to stay at the Sundown ranch?

His gut reaction was to say no. But each time he denied it, he sensed he was lying to himself in an effort to avoid potential heartache for Hilly or himself. And the more he denied it, the more he realized that the answer he was avoiding was definitely: yes.

Beside him Logan never stopped talking. He was easily the most garrulous, good-natured man Blue had ever encountered. He was like an overgrown child, enjoying every moment of life to its fullest; and though his constant laughter and boring jokes got on Blue's nerves, he had to admit that it was impossible not to like the man. He was, Blue realized, everything that he, Blue, wasn't. Tall, handsome, engaging, and seemingly without malice toward anyone, the only possible reason to dislike Hunt Logan was because he was too perfect!

Blue, who cherished silence more than most, tuned Logan out for much of the ride. But as night approached, bringing darkness to the valley, Blue saw lights glittering on the distant horizon. Guessing they were nearing the ranch, he decided it was time to get some questions answered. 'These rustlers you're dealing with,' he said to Logan, 'have you got any idea who they are or who's behind them?'

'Not a clue. One thing's for certain however, none of my neighbors are involved.'

'How can you be so sure?'

''Cause we're like one big happy family. We always stop and chew the gristle when we see each other, we worry about how our livestock's doing, and if one of us doesn't have enough grain stored to last through winter, then the rest of us pitch in and carry them until the hard times are over. We even invite each other to cookouts. So you see, there'd be no reason for one of us to turn rogue. On top of that, all of us have had cattle or horses stolen from time to time, so it's not like one spread has received any special favors from the rustlers.'

'Maybe that's all part of the plan?'

'Plan?'

'To throw the law and all the ranchers off the scent?'

'Scent of what?'

'The identity of whoever it is that's secretly trying to buy up the whole valley.'

Logan frowned. 'Who said anyone was trying to buy up the whole valley?'

'No one. Just a guess.'

'But who'd want to do that? This valley's big enough for everyone.'

'There's always someone who wants more. Otherwise, there'd be no such thing as greed.'

Logan shrugged, unconvinced. 'Anything's possible, I reckon. But I'd still vouch for all my neighbors. And I'd know they'd do the same for me.' He paused and shook his head in bewilderment. 'I tell you, *amigo*, this rustling business has got me and everyone else completely baffled.'

'What about the sheriff?' Blue said. 'Has he rounded up a posse and tried to hunt them down?'

'Sure. More than once. And always with the same result: he returns empty-handed.'

'Maybe he hasn't tried hard enough?'

'I wish that was the case. But in all fairness to Todd Roper, he's done everything we asked him to, and more, and still hasn't been able to throw a rope over the rustlers.'

'Sounds like you're chasing ghosts.'

'For all we ever see of them, we may as well be.'

'Horses ain't ghosts,' Blue said. He squeezed his forehead in an effort to lessen the pain of his headache before adding: 'They leave hoof-prints and hoof-prints don't just disappear.'

'These do. Once the rustlers reach the hills, it's like they vanish into thin air. I know that's impossible,' Logan said quickly, 'but, dammit, that's what happens. I know that for a fact 'cause I've ridden with the posse a few times and seen the results first hand.' He gave a long frustrated sigh before adding: 'I tell you, it's got us all licked.'

'Does that mean you and Hilly will be selling out like the homesteaders are doing?'

'No. We're staying put no matter what. Why? Do you think we should?'

'What I think doesn't matter.'

'I'd still like your opinion.'

Blue shrugged. 'Reckon it depends on what risks you're willing to take, especially with Miss Hilly to protect.'

'Go on.'

'Way I see it, you got two options: sell

and take a big loss or stay and shoot it out with these masked gunmen every night.'

Logan abruptly reined up and eyed Blue questioningly. 'Who you been talking to?'

'No one.'

'Don't give me that. Only a few of us know about the masked gunmen and you ain't one of them.'

'So?'

'So you asked me to lay my cards on the table, now I'm asking you to do the same.'

Blue chewed on that briefly then said: 'Mayor Colton. He contacted me and asked for my help. Said, the Council would pay my fee and expenses if I could get rid of a gang of masked gunmen that were forcing everyone to sell their land. And now, after listening to you, I figure the rustlers and the masked gunmen are one and the same.'

Logan sighed, resigned.

'Sounds like you do too.'

Logan nodded grudgingly. 'Makes

sense,' he agreed. 'So does something else now.'

'What's that?'

'You.'

'Me?'

'I could never figure out how come an old hand like yourself, someone who knows better, would let himself get lost in a desert hot enough to fry your brains.'

'I wasn't lost,' Blue said. 'Not before that cougar jumped me.'

'I know that now. You were on your way here.'

'Right.'

'And then what? Once you got here, I mean?'

'I would've let the mayor know I was in town, got a room and started nosing around until something or someone led to the gunmen.'

'No surprises there.'

'No, but what does surprise me is that the mayor didn't tell you I was coming.'

'That would've been mighty difficult.'

'Meaning?'

'Dave Colton's dead.'

'The mayor's dead?' Blue said, shocked. 'When? How?'

'Three days ago. Shot himself in the head.'

'Suicide?'

Logan nodded grimly. 'Left a note saying life wasn't worth living without his beloved Eunice — that was his wife, Eunice-Mae — by his side. Everyone was shocked, of course, because recently Dave seemed to have gotten over her death. But obviously he hadn't.' Logan sadly shook his head. 'Just goes to show you, doesn't it. What folks are capable of, I mean.' He snapped the reins and the horse broke into a brisk canter.

Blue thought about the mayor's letter. Why would he ask for help if he'd planned to kill himself? It didn't make sense and Blue was sufficiently troubled by it to ask: 'If the mayor hadn't left a note, would you still have believed he committed suicide?'

Logan shrugged. 'Funny you should say that, *amigo*. I've asked myself the same thing over and over.'

'And?'

'Well, much as I didn't want to believe Dave had taken the short way home, I could never explain away his note. No matter how I tried, the damn thing kept haunting me until I finally had to go along with everyone else and admit that Dave pulled the trigger.'

'Ever consider that maybe he didn't write the note?'

'I wish that was an option.'

'Why ain't it?'

'Because there was no getting past his handwriting. One look and I knew he'd written it.'

'Couldn't someone have copied his handwriting?'

'No one in San Dimas. Dave had a very flowery, distinctive hand. Like what you'd expect from an English professor or one of those poet fellas. Everyone in town could recognize it. Especially after he became mayor. Then

Dave not only had to sign lots of official documents, he also was a great one for writing memos. He sent them to everyone. And even though he sometimes didn't sign them, we all knew who they were from just by the handwriting. It was that unique.'

Blue was silent for the longest time. Beside him Logan was itching to talk but had the sense to keep quiet and not prod this strangely enigmatic man. But finally it got too much for him and he said: 'Any more questions?'

'Just one: When did you find out I once worked for the Cattlemen's Association?'

Caught off-guard by the question, Logan tried to hide his surprise and failed miserably. 'W-What makes you say that?' he stammered. 'I — I — m-mean — '

Blue cut him off. 'Spare me the lip-dancing, Hunt. If you want me to get rid of these rustlers or masked gunmen, I need straight answers and I need them now.'

'Okay, okay . . . ' Logan thought a moment before continuing. 'Recently.'

'Who told you?'

'No one. It was just by accident. I was in Abilene a little while back and these cattlemen I knew invited me to join them in a game of stud. I'd played with them before, so I agreed. During the game the conversation got around to rustling and how since the War it had increased ten-fold, and your name came up.'

'Go on.'

'One of players, Jim Hollis, who runs beef up from Waco, said he knew an easy cure but, like all cures, it had some nasty side-effects.'

'Like, what?'

'Casualties of war, is how he put it. And when I asked him if he meant fatal casualties, he said: 'When the recipe calls for Egan Blue, what other kind of casualties are there?' And everybody laughed.'

Blue said grimly: 'I'm glad they found me so amusing.'

99

'Don't get me wrong,' Logan said hastily. 'It wasn't that kind of laugh. It was more of a nervous laugh. You know? Like they were glad you weren't after them.'

They had almost reached the lights they'd seen earlier. Squinting, Blue made out the silhouettes of a ranch house, barn, some smaller outer buildings and several corrals. And, as they got closer, he saw well-armed men patrolling the fence-in-property.

'Friendly little place,' he said. 'I've seen Army posts that weren't as well-guarded.'

'Now you know how bad it's gotten,' Logan said. 'Without these gunnies we'd lose half our livestock overnight.'

One of the gunmen approached, ready to shoot. Then seeing it was Logan, he lowered his rifle, saying: 'Sorry, boss. Didn't recognize you in that girly rig.'

'Don't apologize, Lee,' Logan said. 'That's what I'm paying you for.' He waited until the man had unlatched the gate then drove on through and reined up outside the barn.

Another gunman approached, asking: 'You all done for the night, boss?'

'Yeah. And be sure to grain him 'fore you put him up, okay?' Logan jumped down and came around to Blue's side, ready to help him down.

Blue ignored Logan's outstretched hand and stiffly got down from the buggy.

Logan shrugged off Blue's mild snub and turned to the gunman. 'This is Egan Blue, Marty. He'll be staying with us for a spell. Pass the word to the others. Tell them he has free range of the place.'

'Sure, boss.' The gunman started unhitching the horse. But as Logan led Blue to the house, he looked after them and whistled softly. 'Egan Blue,' he said, faintly awed. 'So that's what death on the hoof looks like?'

15

Hilly, having heard them ride up, met them at the front door. She'd swapped her boy's shirt and jeans for a yellow gingham dress that matched her sun-streaked hair, and Blue felt an emotional rush as they shook hands and she invited him in.

'I'm so glad you accepted my offer,' she exclaimed. 'I was worried you'd think it was forward of me and refuse. But now that you're here, I promise I'll do everything I can to make you comfortable, no matter how brief your stay is.'

'It may not be so brief,' Logan said before Blue could reply. 'I told him about the rustlers and the way we left it was, once he's healed he might help us hunt them down.'

Hilly frowned, as if displeased, and said: 'I hope you don't think that's why

I invited you to stay here, because nothing could be farther from the truth, Mr. Blue.'

Blue gave a rare smile. 'Name's Egan, remember?'

'I'm sorry, I — '

'And, no, I don't think that's why you invited me. Logan, here, made it real clear that it was his idea.'

'Good,' Hilly said, relieved. 'Well, I'm sure you're tired after the long ride out here. Why don't I show you your room, so you can rest up before dinner?'

'If it's all right with you,' Blue said, 'I'd like to wash up first.'

'Of course. Would you show him where the pump is, honey?' she said to Logan.

'Be happy to. This way,' he told Blue.

Behind the house, in the cool darkness, Logan lit a smoke and watched as Blue stripped to the waist and washed off the trail dirt.

'You don't know it,' he said, handing Blue a towel. 'But you're getting what her stepdad, Owen, used to call the

Royal Treatment.'

'Meaning?'

'Hilly. She doesn't usually take a shine to folks like she has to you. 'Least, not until she's got to know them inside and out.'

Blue stopped drying himself and looked squarely at Logan. 'You okay with that?'

'Sure. Why wouldn't I be?'

'Just asking.' Blue finished toweling off, put on his shirt and buckled on his gun-belt. 'A fella who's getting ready to tie the knot tends to be edgy about who his girl does and doesn't take a shine to. And I'm going to have enough problems dealing with these rustlers or masked gunmen, without having to worry about watching my back.'

'You don't have to worry about me,' Logan assured. 'Not when it comes to Hilly. We've been sweethearts since before her stepdad died.'

'Now you mention it, how did Owen die?' Blue asked.

'Passed in his sleep.'

'Lucky man. Not waking up one morning beats the hell out of a bullet in the belly.'

'Amen,' said Logan. He stubbed out his smoke and led Blue back into the house.

16

Logan was as good as his word. When Blue came down to breakfast the next morning, he glanced out the window and saw his horse tied to the rail outside the front door.

Cookie had just brought a stack of flapjacks, eggs and bacon to the table and Blue, after promising to be right back, ducked out the front door. On seeing him the pinto snorted and pawed the dirt.

'It's good to see you, too,' Blue said, rubbing the pinto's proudly arched neck. 'But a word of warning: enjoy your rest while you can. I got an uneasy feeling we won't be sticking around too long — ' He broke off as he heard a noise behind him. Drawing his gun, he whirled around and was surprised to see a familiar face looking at him.

'W-What the devil are you doing

here?' he asked, holstering his gun.

'We're neighbors,' Maddy said, thumbing in the direction of the hills.

Blue squinted and in the far-off distance saw a cabin near the foothills.

'That's a fair piece to walk, Maddy, or did you hitch a ride?'

The albino girl beamed. 'You 'membered my name,' she said, delighted.

'I remember the names of everyone who helps me.'

'Why's that?'

'In case they ever need my help. Do you remember my name?'

'Egan Blue,' Maddy said. ''Leastwise, that's you told Mrs. Strazinsky it was.'

'You do pay attention, don't you?' Blue said, impressed.

'Only when I'm with folks I like and I like you, Mr. Blue. That's a fact.'

'Maddy!' a voice exclaimed behind them. 'What're you doing here?'

Blue and Maddy turned and saw Logan approaching.

'Well, I ain't stealing eggs,' she said, bristling, 'so don't think I am.'

Logan chuckled. But Blue saw a hard glint in his eyes and realized there was some kind of history between these two.

'You can have all the eggs you want,' Logan said affably. 'All you got to do is ask. It's when you take them without asking that I object to — '

'When Mr. Owen was alive,' Maddy interrupted, 'I didn't have to ask him. He let me come over anytime and take as many eggs as I wanted. That's a fact.'

'Well, I'm not Mr. Owen,' Logan said. 'He had his way of doing things, I got mine.'

'I liked his way better. I liked *him* better than you, too,' Maddy said before Logan could reply. 'He was kind and friendly to everyone. And he didn't hire no gunmen to drive folks out of the valley or try to steal miners' claims — '

'Now you're talking nonsense,' Logan said. 'You know perfectly well the men working for me are to protect our livestock from rustlers.'

'Liar,' Maddy said fiercely. 'Those gunmen *are* the rustlers. And they're the masked gunmen, too — '

'Maddy!' Logan said angrily. 'Dammit, child, that's enough! Stealing eggs is one thing, making up lies just to hurt people — '

'They ain't lies,' Maddy insisted. 'It's true and I can prove it. And that's a fact!'

Blue, who'd been listening, said quietly: 'How?'

'Oh, for God's sake, Egan,' exclaimed Logan. 'Don't encourage the little brat!'

Blue ignored him. 'How can you prove it?' he asked Maddy.

''Cause I seen 'em one night when they wasn't wearing their masks.'

'Where?'

'Up in the hills near my uncle's mine. It was dark and they was lighting their torches and putting on their masks, getting ready to burn Mr. Haskins out.'

'How do you know they were going after Mr. Haskins?' demanded Logan.

''Cause I heard them say his name and how they was going to scare him.'

'And these men you saw,' Blue said,

'they're the same men that work here?'

'Yeah. Most of 'em.'

'You're absolutely sure?'

''Course I am. And that's a fact.'

'Then you should have no trouble pointing them out. Look around, Maddy, and tell me if you see any of them now.'

Maddy gazed about her at the gunmen patrolling the fences. Suddenly she pointed at one of them, saying: 'Him! And him, too,' she added, pointing at another gunman.

'What about the other men?' Logan demanded. 'Like those two there?' He indicated two gunmen emerging from the barn. 'Did you see them lighting torches as well?'

'Yeah,' Maddy said emphatically. 'They was there all right!'

'When was this?' Logan said. 'That you saw them, I mean?'

'Last week.'

'What day last week — do you remember?'

'Yeah. Wednesday. I know 'cause my

uncle was working by his mine and found a bunch of nuggets in his sluice box that day. And that's a fact.'

'Wednesday, eh? That's very interesting.' Logan turned to Blue. 'What'd I tell you? Lies. Pure lies.'

'I ain't lying!' Maddy screamed. 'I ain't! I ain't!'

'Is that so?' Logan said. 'Then perhaps you can explain how these two men were in two places at once?'

'What do you mean?'

Ignoring her, Logan said smugly to Blue: 'Emmett and Leland were in Denver for the last two weeks picking up well-drilling equipment. And don't take just my word for it, ask Hilly. She told them while they were there to pick up a dress she'd ordered from a catalog. So you see,' he told Maddy, 'you're lying when you say you saw them lighting torches and putting on their masks. Just like you're lying about the other men. They're gunmen, yes, and they do work for me. But they're only here to protect the livestock, and our lives if necessary, from rustlers.'

Maddy shifted her feet uncomfortably, silent for once.

Logan gave her a patronizing smile. 'Look, just to prove I don't bear any grudges or hard feelings toward you, I'm willing to forget this little ruckus if you are. But from now on, Maddy, stop lying about my men. One day someone might actually believe you and who knows what the consequences could be. Do you understand?'

Again, Maddy shifted uncomfortably and kept her eyes lowered.

'Good,' Logan said. 'Now, why don't you collect as many eggs you need and then leave. Mr. Blue hasn't had his breakfast yet and I've got a herd to tend to.' Patting her condescendingly on the shoulder, he walked to the corral, where his now-saddled dappled gray awaited him.

Maddy looked at Blue, her milky pink eyes full of tears, and then started away.

'Maddy,' he called out. Then as she

looked back at him: 'Anyone can make a mistake. Doesn't mean you're a liar.'

'I ain't lying,' she said adamantly. 'They was there all right. Maybe not them two, but all the others. That's a fact!' Turning, she ran to the fence, slid under the bottom bar and was quickly up and running again, her white braid flopping behind her like a horse's tail.

Blue sighed, troubled by Maddy's accusations, and started back to the house. Before he reached there, he felt a stabbing pain in his head and again a weakness in his left leg. He had to stop and steady himself before slowly limping on.

Logan rode up alongside him. 'Sorry you had to listen to that nonsense. But that's Maddy for you. She's always making up stories about someone. God knows why, but she is and because we love her and feel sorry for her, we all put up with it.'

Blue nodded, but didn't say anything.

'Later,' Logan went on, 'when you're

all done eating, if you're up to it, have one of the boys bring you out to the herd. I haven't told Hilly yet, but we were hit again last night and I want to see how much beef they made off with.' He wheeled his beautiful dappled gray stallion around and rode through the gate, out into the valley.

Blue gazed thoughtfully after him, trying to make up his mind about the man.

17

Blue was wolfing down his second serving of scrambled eggs and ham when Hilly joined him at the breakfast table. Though she was wearing cowboy boots, jeans and a man's denim shirt, he thought she looked radiant and quickly reminded himself that she was soon to be married.

'Good morning, Egan,' she said breezily.

''Morning.'

Hilly waved away the plate of food that Cookie brought to her, saying, 'Just coffee, please,' and then sat across from Blue. 'How did you sleep?' she asked. 'I'm afraid that bed isn't too comfortable, and being so sore, you probably were up half the night.'

'I hate to pass up your sympathy,' he said, smiling, 'but I slept just fine.'

'Really?' She studied him with big

hazel eyes that seemed to see right through him. 'You don't have to pretend just to make me feel better, you know. Over the years, when Owen's guests stayed with us, I had to sleep in that bed. And though I'm sure it's softer than the beds at the Palomar, I still woke up feeling like I'd wrestled a bear and lost.'

Blue chuckled. 'Soft or hard,' he said, 'it beats sleeping on the ground.'

'Is that what you were doing when the cougar attacked you?'

Blue shook his head and briefly explained what happened.

Impressed, Hilly said: 'You and the pinto must have a very special bond. Most horses would have bolted.'

'Truth is,' Blue said, 'he was probably on the verge of bolting too.'

'Really?'

'Sure. But then he was smart enough to realize the next fella who owned him might be even harder on him than me, so he stomped the daylights out of that cat.'

He expected Hilly to laugh. Instead, she said seriously: 'Do you always do that?'

'Do what?'

'Make yourself out to be the child nobody wants?'

'Wasn't aware I did,' Bluc said. 'As for me and the pinto, you're right: we've bonded some over the years. It's just that — '

'You feel uncomfortable talking about it?'

Blue met her gaze without flinching. 'You don't hold back, do you?'

'I say what I'm thinking, if that's what you mean?' When he didn't answer, she said: 'Is it because I'm a woman?'

'I'm not following you.'

She gave him a probing look before answering. 'You know it's funny. Well, sad really. Men expect other men to say what's on their mind and think nothing of it when they do. But when women do it, men act like we're speaking out of turn, challenging them, you might say, and they start hemming and hawing and looking everywhere but at us, like you're doing now. Why is that, Egan? Can you tell me? I'd really like to know.'

Blue wished he had a cigarette. Life and its problems were always easier to handle when he was smoking. Taking a drag, feeling the smoke hit his lungs, even exhaling, they were all things that gave a man time to think of what to say next.

'Well?'

Trapped, Blue said slowly: 'I don't reckon I know the answer to that, ma'am.'

'Hilly.'

'Hilly. But I suspect it's 'cause most women — the ones I've known anyway — prefer it that way.'

'Being shadows, you mean?'

Again he wished he had a smoke.

'Is it because you feel threatened?'

'No, ma'a — Hilly, that ain't it at all. As boys, we're just doing what we were told to do by our folks, while growing up. They taught us how men were supposed to act and how women was supposed to act. Hammered it into us until that's all we knew. Right or wrong, that's just the way it is. And when you come up against a woman who — '

'Doesn't act like you expect,' Hilly interrupted, 'it throws you for a loop? Right?'

Blue nodded. Then, anxious to end this awkward conversation, he said: 'I don't mean to be rude, ma'am — Hilly, but Logan's expecting me to ride out to the herd. So if you don't mind, I'll be moving along.'

'Go right ahead,' Hilly said, gulping her coffee and rising. 'I have to talk to Hunt myself, so unless you object, I'll ride with you.'

'You're the boss,' Blue said simply.

18

The herd was grazing at the north end of the valley. As Hilly and Blue rode up, he judged there was about eight hundred head. It wasn't a large number when compared to the great herds that were driven up from Texas to one of the railheads in Kansas or Missouri, but it was still larger than the smaller ranches could muster.

It also supported the rumors Blue had heard in town about how the night raiders were being paid by Logan, on Hillary Darby's orders, to get scare off the owners of the small ranches so that her ever-enlarging herd had more room to graze. Blue hated to think the rumors were true. But the longer he stuck around and the more familiar he became with the land disputes over the shrinking free range, the harder it was for him to dismiss the rumors as sour grapes.

The three night hawks spotted Blue and Hilly approaching the herd and two of them rode out to greet their boss. Logan wasn't one of them and when Hilly asked where he was, one night hawk replied that Logan and three other men had taken off right after sunup in pursuit of rustlers who under the cover of darkness had cut out twenty head and ridden off before anyone could stop them.

'Which direction did they go?' Blue asked.

'Toward the hills,' the night hawk replied. 'But they got a good jump on you.'

'You going after them?' Hilly said to Blue.

'Unless you tell me not to.'

Resigned, Hilly shook her head. 'Take as many men as you think you'll need.'

'No men,' he replied. 'But I could use two extra horses.'

'Cut them out of the *remuda*,' she said, adding: 'You don't have to do this, you know. We'll survive without twenty head.'

'If it was going to end there, I'd agree with you. But it won't. Not once they figure you're easy pickings. First twenty, then fifty and then God knows how many the time after that.'

She knew he was right. She also saw the resolve in Blue's gray eyes and knew better than argue. 'Take care of yourself,' she said, 'I need you.'

She spoke with such caring it could have been mistaken for affection, and Blue wasn't sure how to respond.

'I'll hold you to that,' he said finally. He then whirled his horse around and rode toward the string of unsaddled horses grazing at the edge of the herd.

They snorted and became skittish as he approached. Blue waved to one of the night hawks to help him. The rider obliged. Together they cut out two leggy, deep-chested horses, a red roan and a sorrel, roped and bridled them but didn't saddle them.

Blue then swung up on the back of

the sorrel, grasped the reins of his horse and the roan, and rode off in the direction of the hills.

He rode hard, pushing the sorrel to its limits for a several miles. Then as it started laboring, he didn't bother to stop but vaulted onto the back of the roan, at the same time keeping hold of the reins of the pinto while releasing the sorrel. It stood there, flanks heaving, watching him ride off. Then instinctively it started back toward the *remuda.*

Blue rode the roan into the ground. When it began to falter, he leaped onto the pinto and released the roan. Like the sorrel, the roan headed in the direction of the ranch.

'If you ever felt like running,' Blue told the pinto, 'now's the time, partner!'

The pinto responded. Flattening its ears, it settled into a long-striding gallop. As Blue leaned low over its neck, he felt the wind battering his cheeks and his eyes watering.

Fortunately, the trail was well-used

and reasonably smooth. There were very few settlements beside the trail, and whenever Blue came to one he skirted the scattered buildings and picked up the trail on the other side. With no extra horses, Blue held the pinto to an easy, mile-consuming lope. He knew how far the pinto could travel this way and was fairly confident that he could overtake Logan and possibly the rustlers before they got too deep into the hills. Fortunately, the sun was on his side. It was behind him. Better still, as if favoring him and the pinto, it did not break through the early morning overcast . . . keeping the temperature much cooler.

Time and the miles slid past. Blue didn't know how far he'd traveled when he caught sight of four riders ahead. They had no cattle with them and one of the horses was a dappled gray, indicating it was Logan and the men he'd taken with him. Their horses were sweat-caked and when they heard Blue coming up behind them, they looked back and on Logan's orders reined up to wait for him.

Logan looked irritated to see him. 'If Hilly's sent you to bring us back, you wore out your horse for nothing.'

'She didn't,' Blue replied. 'I'm throwing in with you.'

For an instant it looked like Logan was going to refuse Blue's help.

'You hired me for my gun, remember?' Blue reminded.

Logan relented, said, 'Suit yourself,' rejoined his men and they all rode on.

They rode deeper into the hills. Overhead, Hawks drifting on the thermals kept them company. Other than a disturbed whitetail that suddenly bounded across the trail in front of them, there was no sign of life on the ground. Soon after they saw the deer, natural caves appeared on some of the slopes and here and there several narrow canyons split off from the main trail.

Logan seemed to grow tense. Blue, watching him, dropped his hand to his six-gun, ready to draw if they were threatened. After a mile or so, Logan reined up at the mouth of one of the larger canyons, dismounted and knelt to examine the countless hoof prints in the dirt. Shortly, he straightened up, remounted and said to his men: 'I count five riders and the rest of the prints belong to cattle — most likely ours.'

'The odds are even then,' said one of the men, an edgy string-bean named Addison.

'Unless there's a bunch more rustlers already holed up in the canyon,' another man, Sal Clements, reminded.

'Almost got to be,' remarked the third man, Lew Carey. 'I mean, five men can't account for all the rustling that's been going on lately.'

'How 'bout it, boss?' Addison asked. 'You figure we're riding into a hornet's nest?'

'Only one way to find out,' Logan replied. 'One of us has got to go on ahead and scout things out. Don't worry,' he added as the men swapped uneasy glances, 'I led you into this, it's only right I take the risk.'

The men looked relieved. But Blue thought Logan seemed too eager to sacrifice himself and wondering why, said: 'I'll go with you. Someone's got to watch your back.'

Logan hesitated, again on the verge of refusing Blue's help, then said: 'Okay, but no gunplay unless I give the word. I don't want you starting a range war that could end up killing off half the folks in the valley, not to mention getting our ranches torched.'

'That's fine with me,' Blue said. 'Lead the way.'

19

The two of them rode cautiously into the canyon. Blue let Logan take the lead but kept the pinto's head level with the flank of Logan's dappled gray, neither man saying a word.

On both sides of them the rocky hillsides grew steeper and closer. The trail narrowed and became more winding; more dangerous. Blue kept his eye on Logan, sensing the foreman wasn't being straight with him. Simultaneously he kept looking up at both walls of the canyon, which now towered above them and were so close that he and Logan had to ride single file.

Knowing a lookout could easily kill them by causing a rockslide Blue grabbed his Winchester and rested it across the saddle horn. He kept one finger on the trigger so that at the first sign of danger he could snap off a shot and perhaps kill the lookout before he could start the slide.

Shortly, Logan reined up and signaled for Blue to stop. 'We're almost there,' he said quietly. 'Just ahead the canyon opens up into a meadow. That's where the rustlers must be holding our cattle.'

'If you're right, how do you want to play this?'

'Depends on how many rustlers there are.'

'What about the men?' Blue said. 'Shouldn't one of us go back and get them?'

'Forget the men and worry about yourself, *amigo*.' Logan drew his six-gun as he spoke and aimed it at Blue's belly. 'It's your life that's on the line.'

'Funny,' Blue said contemptuously, 'I was wondering when you'd make your play.'

'Was I that obvious?'

'Like a candle in the dark. What's this all about anyway?'

'Choices.'

'And I'm down to my last one, that it?'

'Exactly.'

Blue laughed softly. 'Quit running a bluff, Hunt. If you'd wanted me dead, you could have easily killed me by now. So, let's get down to chips. What do you want from me?'

'First,' Logan said, 'Maddy was right: the masked gunmen and rustlers *are* the men working at the ranch. But I reckon you'd already guessed that?'

'It crossed my mind,' Blue admitted. 'And you, you're calling the shots?'

'Yes.'

'I'm guessing that Miss Hilly ain't involved in this?'

''Course not! She'd never go along with anything even remotely illegal, even though she knows we need more grass if the herd's ever going to grow like she wants.'

Blue thought a moment before asking: 'Who's pocketing the money from the stolen beef?'

130

'I am. But I intend to pay it all back to Hilly as a wedding present,' Logan said, 'plus interest. You can take my word to the bank on that.'

Blue said only: 'Which brings us back to me. What do you need my gun for?'

'To kill one of the rustlers who's gone rogue on me.'

'Why don't you shoot him?'

'He's too fast. Ungrateful bastard! I saved his neck from getting stretched, and now he's trying to buffalo me and the men.'

'He must be doing a hell of a job,' Blue said, 'else I wouldn't be here.'

'Save your sarcasm. Will you do it?'

'So long as you meet my price.'

'A thousand dollars?'

'In cash.'

'Then we're in accord,' Logan said, holstering his gun. 'C'mon, let's go meet the boys.' He urged his horse ahead and Blue followed on the pinto.

20

As they rode out of the canyon, into a small enclosed meadow, Logan signaled to the two lookouts on the rocks above them. The men lowered their rifles and waved them on.

'Ride alongside me,' Logan told Blue, 'and keep your hand away from your gun. These men are all murderers and thieves who believe in shooting first and asking questions afterwards.'

'I'm sounding more like an angel every day,' Blue said dryly.

Logan made a scoffing sound. 'God help heaven if that's true.'

Together, they guided their horses through the cattle that were grazing all around them. The meadow was oval, studded with oak trees and there was a creek running through the far end of it. Near the creek a large, ground-level cave showed in the rock-strewn hillside.

Gunmen lounged around outside the cave, some of them sitting drinking coffee beside a campfire. They were all hard-looking unshaven men with cold, unforgiving eyes, and as one they turned and watched as Blue and Logan rode toward them.

As Blue got closer he recognized some of the faces watching him. He hadn't ridden with any of the men, or called them out, and yet he could tell by the way they looked at him that they knew about his reputation. He wondered which of the gunmen he would end up shooting, and if what Logan had said about the man was true or just Logan's excuse for getting rid of someone who was trying to challenge him for leadership. Either way, Blue reminded himself, the outcome would be the same: another thousand dollars toward restoring his family home to its glorious past . . . and another dead gunman!

While still out of earshot of the rustlers, Logan said quietly: 'That's him

. . . the tall yahoo in the red shirt and brown hat? See him? Standing outside the cave on the left, smoking a cigar . . . wearing that fancy two-gun rig?'

Blue picked out the man Logan described. 'Mite young in the tooth to be running scared of, ain't he?'

'Tell me that after you've drawn down on him — *if* you're still standing.'

'Maybe I should raise my price?'

Logan shot Blue a sidelong look and saw that the gunman was faintly smiling.

They were clear of the cattle now and almost up to the men. They were all sizing up Blue; especially the men who knew of his reputation. Dismounting, Logan and Blue tied up their horses and joined the men at the campfire.

'For any of you who don't already know,' Logan told them, 'this is Egan Blue. He's joining us.'

Blue and the men exchanged curt nods. The other rustlers who'd been lounging at the entrance to the cave now closed in to hear Logan's words.

'As you know, boys, I'm getting married soon. While I'm on my honeymoon, I've hired Blue to run things for me.'

'How's that going to work?' asked one rustler.

'You saying we're supposed to take orders from him?' asked another.

'That's exactly what I'm saying.' Logan looked at the faces surrounding him. 'Any of you got a problem with that?'

The men shuffled awkwardly, muttering and swapping looks with each other, but none of them disagreed. Then Will Hobbs, the tall young gunman Logan had earlier pointed out to Blue, stepped forward.

'Yeah,' he said sullenly. 'I do.'

'You do what?' Blue replied before Logan could answer.

'I got a problem with taking orders from you, mister.'

At once the men nervously stepped back, out of the line of fire.

'This problem,' Blue said softly, 'is it

that you're deaf or too stupid to understand what I'm saying?'

There was a deadly silence as everyone waited to see how Hobbs would respond.

He didn't let them down. Happy to be challenged, he hitched up his crossed gun belts and dropped his hands to the ivory-handled Colts tucked in the low-slung holsters.

'Mister,' he grinned, 'I've heard you're plenty fast with that .44 of yourn, but today you're overmatched.'

About to reply Blue felt one of his stabbing pains in his head and wondered if he'd gotten himself into a gunfight that he couldn't win. But then, just as suddenly, the pain diminished, became tolerable and he said in a dangerous whisper: 'Prove it, *sonny*.'

Stung, Hobbs lost his grin and went for his guns.

Blue did the same.

The thunderous booms as both men fired were too close to tell apart.

Blue felt a sharp burning sensation as

one of Hobbs' bullets tore through his side.

He never took his eyes off Hobbs, who lurched backward as he was hit. He stood there for a moment, a shocked look on his youthful, freckled face. Then he sank to his knees, guns dropping from his lifeless hands, head slumped down, and died.

The men had never seen anyone die on their knees before. Surprised, they stared at Hobbs, all wondering if he was actually dead. It was only when Blue holstered his gun, turned and limped to his horse that the men recovered and rushed to examine Hobbs.

'He's dead all right,' one man said. He pointed at the blood darkening Hobbs' red shirt over his heart. 'Put one in him dead center.'

The other men nodded, murmuring among themselves, some of them giving Blue sidelong looks as if to acknowledge that he had lived up to his deadly reputation.

'Bury him,' Logan told the men.

'And don't bother about a marker.' He joined Blue, who was leaned against the pinto pulling out his shirt. 'We got a fella here, Doc Fleming, who once practiced in Cheyenne. He's old and mostly drunk, but this early in the day he should be sober enough to cut that lead out of you.'

Blue gently probed at his bleeding wound. 'He won't have to,' he said. 'Bullet went right through. Little whisky and a few stitches and I'll be like new again.'

'We'll celebrate when Doc Fleming agrees with you,' Logan said. 'Come on. I'll take you to him.'

He helped Blue into the cave. The men gathered in the main chamber of the smoke-filled cave, stared at Blue as he limped in with a mixture of fear and grudging respect.

'Don't mind them,' Logan said as he led Blue to the back of the cave. 'They'll come around once they know you gunned down Hobbs. They all hated the SOB.'

Logan and Blue halted beside a gaunt, straggly-haired man lying on a pile of dirty blankets. Though only in his late fifties, his lifelong addiction to whisky made him look twenty years older. His eyes were bloodshot and almost hidden behind puffy bags, his skin was sallow and heavily wrinkled, and the sagging corners of his thin-lipped mouth gave him a look of permanent despair.

'Doc,' Logan said bending over the man, 'this is Egan Blue.'

The man, Dr. Noah Fleming, stared blearily at Logan but didn't respond.

Logan reached down, pulled him into a sitting position and gently but firmly shook him until the man blinked and seemed to come out of whatever stupor he'd been in.

'Doc, you hear me? My pal, here, has been shot and needs your help.'

Fleming reacted as if hearing Logan for the first time. 'W-Wheresh my bag?' he slurred. 'I need my damn bag, Logan. Y'unnerstand? I gotta have my bag.'

'It's right here,' Logan handed him an old black leather bag and helped pulled him up. 'Can you stand, Doc?'

''C-Course I can stan — ' Fleming swayed, off-balance, and would have fallen but for Logan's steadying hand. 'H-Help me to my op-p-p'rating table.'

'Sure, doc, sure.' Logan picked up the frail little physician and carried him to a flat blood-stained rock that served as a chair-and-table. Gently setting Fleming on the narrow end, legs straddling the rock, Logan grabbed the doctor's shoulders and kept him in a sitting position while Blue stood beside him.

Fleming fumbled around in his bag, muttering curses, and finally pulled out a reel of suture thread and a long curved needle.

'I'll do that for you, doc,' Logan said. Taking the thread and needle from Fleming, he walked to a flaming torch stuck in a crevice and by its light threaded the needle. 'Here you go,' he said, handing it back to Fleming.

Then as the doctor stared blankly at it:

'Hang on a minute, doc, while I get the whisky.' Logan went to the fire, took a half-empty bottle of whisky from one of the men and returned beside Blue, who'd removed his shirt. Logan first poured whisky over the needle, sterilizing it, then poured some over the still-bleeding wound just above Blue's hip.

Blue winced, grasped the bottle and took a long swallow before returning it to Logan. 'Okay, go ahead,' he told Fleming. 'But sew it up good, doc. I don't want it to rip open when I start riding.'

'You heard the man,' Logan added. 'Get to it, sawbones.'

21

Despite his befuddled, drunken condition and trembling hands, Fleming somehow managed to concentrate long enough to stitch up Blue's wound. But the strain broke him. As soon as he'd finished and snipped off the remaining thread, he desperately grabbed the whisky bottle from Logan and took a long swig. Then protectively hugging the bottle as if it were a newborn baby, he begged to be taken back to bed.

'How 'bout some food first, doc?' Logan suggested.

If Fleming heard him, he didn't show it. Instead he became highly agitated and again begged to be put to bed. Logan tried to calm him and when that didn't work, he picked Fleming up and carried him to his pile of dirty blankets. He and Blue then left the cave.

Outside, in the bright searing heat,

they walked to their horses.

'When do I get my fee?' Blue said as he tightened the cinch strap under the pinto's belly.

'Tomorrow soon enough?' Logan said.

'Sure.'

'You can ride into town with me and I'll withdraw the money from the bank.'

'Fair enough.'

'One question,' Logan said as they mounted. 'Do you still figure on staying at the ranch, like Hilly wanted?'

'I doubt it.'

'She's going to be mighty hurt.'

'She'll get over it.'

'Yeah, but why upset her in the first place? Like you said, she saved your life so in a way you owe her. 'Sides,' Logan added, 'my offer still goes. Good men are hard to find and when I find one, I'm willing to pay top dollar.'

Blue hesitated, tempted, but at the same time wondered why he was torturing himself when he already knew he was dying.

Misunderstanding Blue's silence, Logan pounced. 'At least stick around long enough to give your wound a chance to heal. If you tear open the stitches, it could get infected and that's the last thing you want.'

Blue knew Logan was right. Besides, he was out of targets to kill. 'Okay,' he said grudgingly. 'But on one condition.'

'Name it.'

'That you put me to work. Charity always sticks in my craw.'

'Don't worry, *amigo,* there's plenty of work to keep an extra hand busy.'

'Just one more thing,' Blue continued, 'as long as I'm at the ranch, they'll be no more rustling. After what Miss Hilly did for me, I can't stand by and see her taken advantage of — even if you do intend to eventually pay her back for the stolen cattle.'

'Deal,' Logan said, adding: 'Tell you what, *amigo.* Just to prove I'm on the level, we'll drive those twenty stolen head back to the ranch. That way, Hilly not only gets her beef back but we'll both come off looking like heroes. How's that sound?'

'Like something I can live with,' Blue said.

'Then let's go round up those cattle.'

The men working at Sundown ranch were surprised to see Blue and Logan driving the stolen beef toward the cattle pen. But they knew better than to question their boss, who'd been known to fire hands that didn't mind their own business.

One of the gunmen hurried to the pen and opened the gate, while two others slapped their hats against their chaps and hollered at the approaching cattle. Their tactics worked. The cattle blindly followed the lead steer into the pen, and when the last cow was safely inside the gunman closed the gate.

Blue and Logan dismounted in front of the house, tied up their horses and went inside.

'Hilly?' Logan called out. 'Honey, where are you?'

'In here,' Hilly replied. 'Working on the books.'

Logan led Blue into the parlor, on through to a smaller adjoining room that Hilly used as her office. She looked up from her desk, smiling, as they entered.

'I've got great news,' Logan said, kissing her on the cheek. 'Egan and I tracked down the stolen cattle. The rustlers had them hidden in a small canyon up in the hills and after we shot it out with them, they high-tailed it out of there, leaving us nothing left to do but drive the cattle back here.'

'That's wonderful,' she exclaimed. Then to Blue: 'I'm very grateful to you, but you shouldn't have risked helping Hunt. Not with that wound of yours. You could've easily reinjured yourself and set your recovery back weeks.'

Blue shrugged and stood there, awkwardly twisting his hat around.

'I told him the exact same thing,' Logan said. 'But he insisted. Said you'd saved his life and this was a small way of paying you back. As it turned out, it was lucky he did.'

'Why's that?' Hilly asked.

''Cause Doc Fleming was holed up with the rustlers.'

'My God, that drunken reprobate?'

'And after we chased them off, he stitched Egan up and — '

Alarmed, Hilly cut him off. 'Egan, you let that old sot stitch up your wound?'

'Yes, ma'am, and he did a fine job of it too.'

Hilly couldn't hide her disbelief. 'I hope to God you sterilized everything first? Otherwise you're sure to get an infection.'

'We did,' Blue assured her.

'Wasted a lot of good whiskey doing it, too,' Logan joked.

Hilly wasn't amused. 'Well, hopefully that cleansed everything,' she said, adding: 'I don't suppose either of you have bothered to eat?'

Logan shook his head and grinned. 'Is that pot roast I smell?' he asked, looking toward the kitchen.

'I don't want to put you to any trouble,' Blue said before Hilly could reply.

'Don't be silly. It's no trouble,' she said. 'There's a whole kettle of it cooking in there. All you two have to do is wash up and we can eat anytime you like.'

'That's good enough for me,' Logan said, grasping Blue's arm. 'C'mon, *amigo*, you ain't lived till you've tasted my girl's pot roast!' He dragged Blue out.

Hilly looked after them, her expression suggesting that she sensed Logan — and maybe Blue, too — had somehow put one over on her.

22

The pot roast tasted even better than it smelled. Hilly served both men large portions, along with plenty of peas and gravy-covered mashed potatoes, and then sat at the table watching them wolf down the food with a delight usually reserved for doting mothers.

'Aren't you going to eat?' Logan asked her.

'I can't. I'm already stuffed. I'll let you in on a little secret,' she confided when Logan and Blue looked puzzled, 'I kept tasting the pot roast as I was cooking it and by the time it was ready, I must've eaten a full meal.'

'Don't you just love her?' Logan said, grinning at Blue. 'I mean, most women would keep that to themselves, but not her. She never holds anything back from me.'

'Don't you believe it,' Hilly laughed.

'There's a whole world of things that you don't know anything about. And that's the way I intend to keep it — '

'Only until we're married,' Logan said. 'Then, you can't hide anything from me.'

'Who says?'

'I do.'

'Ho ho ho.'

'No, no, I'm serious. Ain't that right?' he said to Blue.

'You're asking the wrong person,' Blue said. 'I've never been hitched.'

'Well, it is,' Logan said petulantly. 'And you can take that to the bank.'

'If you believe that,' Hilly said, only half-joking, 'then you're only fooling yourself. Why, soon as you slip that ring on my finger, all bets are off.'

'Oh-ho, so that's the way it's going to be, is it? Well, two can play at that game. Isn't that right?' he said to Blue.

Blue managed to smile but didn't say anything. Though he knew Hilly and Logan were only teasing one another, their intimate needling made him uncomfortable and he would have liked nothing better than to go.

'Leave Egan out of this,' Hilly told Logan. 'Can't you see you're embarrassing him?'

'Hogwalla!' Logan slapped Blue on the back. 'He's not embarrassed, are you, pal? He just ain't one to show his feelings, that's all.'

Hilly, sensing Blue's uneasiness, said: 'How about some more pot roast? And mashed potatoes?'

Blue started to refuse, but Logan cut him off.

'First thing you got to understand if you're going to work here, *amigo*, is you never say no to anything the boss says. And I mean *anything*. She can be a hellcat — '

'Will you stop it?' Hilly exclaimed. 'You're giving him the wrong impression.'

'And if you argue with her,' Logan continued, 'she'll tell cookie to poison your grub.'

Blue, deciding he'd had enough, gave

Hilly his plate, saying: 'If you please, yes.'

Hilly smiled, and took his plate into the kitchen.

'See? What'd I tell you?' Logan laughed. 'She thinks you're special.'

'Why?' Blue said, irked. ''Cause she's getting me a second helping?'

''Cause you got her eating out of your hand,' Logan said. 'I swear to you, *hombre*. In all the years I've known Hilly, I've never seen her be so cordial 'round a stranger.'

Blue didn't reply. He was beginning to dislike Logan and already regretted having agreed to recuperate at the ranch. But he also felt an emotional tie to Hilly and figured he should stay if for no other reason than to protect her from her fiancé for at least as long as he lived.

His thoughts were interrupted by Hilly returning. 'I hope this is enough,' she said, setting his food before him. 'If it isn't, don't hesitate to ask for more.'

'It's plenty, thanks,' Blue said.

'How 'bout a drink?' Logan said, rising and going to the bar. 'I, for one, could use one. Nothing like lead flying 'bout your head to raise a man's thirst.'

He was joking but Hilly wasn't amused. She became upset and after Logan had poured himself three fingers and taken a swallow, she chided: 'I wish you wouldn't take chances like that, Hunt. After all, you have responsibilities around here. I'm depending on you to not only run this ranch but to make sure it runs efficiently and makes a profit — '

'What do you call rounding up twenty head of stolen beef, if not profitable?' Logan snapped. He drained his glass and quickly refilled it. 'Good God, Hilly, this is the first time anyone in the valley has got the better of these rustlers.'

'I know that, Hunt. And I'm proud of you — you and Egan. But what if you'd been killed? You could have, you know. Then what? I'd not only lose my foreman but my fiancé as well!'

'But you didn't lose me,' Logan said. 'And with Egan's help, I got the cattle back and proved — ' He broke off, realizing he'd said too much, and gulped down his whisky.

'Proved what?' Hilly said.

'Nothing,' he said sullenly.

'No, no. Tell me. I'd like to know.'

Logan glared at her but didn't reply.

'That you're worthy of marrying me?'

'Forget it!' he snapped.

'I don't want to forget it,' she said. 'Nor do I want you to keep trying to prove how tough and brave you are just to kick dirt in the face of a dead man.'

Logan whitened with rage. 'I *said*, forget it!'

'No, no, I can't. Not anymore. Not when it may cost me my future husband!'

'Suit yourself, dammit!' Logan poured himself another drink and stormed out before Hilly could stop him.

She sighed, closed her eyes for a moment as if trying to defeat an invisible enemy, and then opened them again and smiled regretfully at Blue.

'I'm sorry you had to witness that, Egan. Washing your dirty linen in public is never a good thing, and to do it in front of you is particularly reprehensible. For that I apologize and hope that you'll forgive me.'

'Nothing to forgive,' Blue said.

'It's just that this problem has been going on for — for years!'

Blue went on eating, wishing Hilly would drop the subject.

'Ever since Hunt started working here in fact. My stepdad was pretty tough on him, as he was with everyone, and Hunt somehow got it into his head that Owen didn't think he was good enough for me. Ever since, he's gone out of his way to prove him wrong.'

Blue sensed she wanted to hear his opinion, maybe even his assurance that she was right about Logan, but instead he wiped his lips on his napkin and got to his feet. 'If you'll excuse me, ma'am, I'd like to put my gear in the bunkhouse — '

'B-But what about your room? I mean aren't you going to sleep here?'

'I reckon it's better if I sleep in the bunkhouse with the rest of the boys,' Blue said.

'I see.' Hurt, Hilly didn't say anything for a moment, then: 'Yes, yes, you're right of course. We don't want them to think I'm playing favorites. Besides, as I said before, that bed in the spare bedroom is hard as a rock and . . . ' Her voice cracked and she turned away so he wouldn't see her tears.

Blue wanted to put his arms around her and beg her not to cry. But he'd been alone too long to be demonstrative, so he just stood there, motionless, unable to comfort her.

Not understanding his silence, Hilly kept her back turned to him as she said, 'G'night, Egan. Sleep well,' and then hurried from the room. He heard her run upstairs and a few moments later, her bedroom door slam.

'Damn,' he said softly. At the same

time he thought: Serves you right, you idiot, for thinking you could be a part of her life. Got no one to blame but yourself. You're only a few steps from the grave, remember? So quit pretending you're normal. Then maybe next time you won't try to be someone you ain't!

Finished punishing himself, he dropped his napkin on the table and went to the bar. There he poured himself a double and downed it in two gulps. Then deciding that the sooner he quit the better, he headed for the spare bedroom to collect his things.

23

Clouds covered the moon and it was dark and cold as Blue carried his gear past the bunkhouse. He'd deliberately left his spurs off and walked as quietly as he could, not wanting to arouse anyone who might ask him where he was going. Ahead, a dozen or more horses stood sleepily together in the far corner of the corral. One of them broke away as Blue approached and hung its head over the gate to greet him.

'I warned you that we mightn't stick around here too long,' Blue whispered as he rubbed the pinto's velvety soft nose. The horse snickered, as if understanding, and stepped back so Blue could unlatch the gate. 'Truth is, though, even I didn't figure we'd be moving on this quick.'

Once he'd saddled and bridled the pinto, Blue fastened on his spurs, mounted and settled his boots into the stirrups. The pinto tensed, expecting to feel the light touch of spurs on its flanks. But Blue couldn't leave without a final look at the house.

Upstairs, above the front door, a light showed in the window of Hilly's bedroom. Blue gazed at it and released a long regretful sigh. Inside, where his heart pumped, he felt a painful ache that he'd never felt before. It hurt more than his gunshot wound; more even than his incessant headaches. Knowing he'd brought it on himself, he cursed himself for daring to think — however briefly — that he belonged somewhere; or, worse, that he stood any chance at all of winning Hilly from Logan. Treacherous as the handsome foreman was, he was still a better catch than a wanted outlaw whose death was imminent!

'Goddamn fool!' Blue said, so suddenly that the pinto flinched. 'That's what you are, Egan Blue. Nothing but a . . . ' Too angry to finish, he dug his spurs into the pinto's flanks. The startled horse broke into a gallop that carried them through the gate, out into the dark desert scrubland.

★ ★ ★

Once he was well clear of the ranch Blue reined in the pinto and rubbed it fondly on the neck. But the horse was still smarting from the sting of the spurs and it ignored Blue and stood there, skin twitching, tail swishing angrily, staring at the distant hills.

Blue, knowing he deserved the stallion's cold shoulder treatment, chuckled and urged the pinto forward with a click of his tongue.

Dark drifting clouds still hid the moon and Blue held the pinto at an easy loping gallop so that it wouldn't accidentally step into a gopher hole and break its leg. A mile or so passed. Then a short distance ahead, in front the hills, Blue saw the outline of a cabin that he remembered belonged to

Maddy's uncle. He guided the pinto to the left, intending to skirt the cabin, but as he did a rifle cracked and a bullet whined past his head.

Startled, Blue quickly reined up, dismounted, grabbed his Winchester and took cover behind some nearby rocks. 'Hey, you in the cabin!' he yelled. 'Hold your fire! I mean you no harm.'

Silence, save for the faint moaning of the wind.

'Did you hear me?' Blue yelled. 'Hold your fire!'

There was muted chatter in the darkness outside the cabin and then Blue heard a familiar voice call out: 'Mr. Blue? Mr. Blue, is that you?'

'Yeah, Maddy, it's me all right!'

'You alone?'

'Yeah.'

'Then come ahead,' Maddy shouted. 'It's a friend of mine,' Blue heard her tell someone. 'Don't shoot at him no more.'

Blue stood up, grasped the pinto's reins and walked slowly toward the cabin. Before he reached it, Maddy came running up to him, clutching an old .22 rifle.

'You ain't winged or nothing, are you?' she asked, concerned. 'I mean, me and my uncle, we didn't know it was you or else we wouldn't have shot at you. That's a fact.'

'It's all right,' Blue said. 'I'm fine.'

'Thank goodness!' Maddy dropped her rifle and hugged him as hard as she could.

For a moment Blue didn't respond. But she felt so good pressed against him that to his surprise, he found himself hugging her back.

'C'mon,' she said, grudgingly releasing him, 'I want you to meet my uncle.'

Blue let her lead him to the cabin. There, outside the front door, stood a tall, dignified, militarily-erect man with a white beard and shoulder-length white hair holding a carbine. In his sixties, he wore red long johns tucked into knee-high boots and had a dark blue Union cavalry greatcoat draped over his shoulders. Blue noticed two gold shoulder boards, each containing eagle's wings, on the coat.

'Uncle, this is Mr. Blue — you know, the man I told you about,' Maddy said.

'Colonel John J. Philo,' her uncle said, offering Blue his hand. 'I've heard a lot about you, mister.'

'I hope some of it was good,' Blue said, shaking hands.

'Pretty much all of it, sir.'

'Call me Egan,' Blue said, adding: 'I'm glad to hear that, Colonel. A man can never have enough good words spoke over him.'

'See, uncle?' Maddy said, glowing. 'I told you me'n him were friends.'

'That you did, girl. That you did.' To Blue, Philo said: 'There's coffee on the stove. You're welcome to a cup if you're a mind to fight off this chill?'

'He'd love a cup,' Maddy said quickly. 'Wouldn't you, Mr. Blue?'

Blue grinned, amused by her eagerness. 'Reckon you're reading my mind, Maddy.'

'Then after you've watered your pony, come inside,' Philo said and entered the cabin.

Blue led the pinto to a nearby water trough. 'Remember what I told you 'bout bloating,' he warned as the horse began drinking thirstily.

The pinto raised its head, shook water all over Blue and then went on drinking.

'Fine! See if I care,' Blue grumbled, and followed Maddy into the cabin.

Inside, the small, low-ceilinged room was neat and clean but felt claustrophobic to a man used to sleeping under the stars. Everything smelled of pipe tobacco and cold bacon grease. A stove with an iron skillet and a coffeepot atop it stood against the rear wall, and nearby a homemade table and chairs sat facing the only window. In one corner was a cot with an old Union Cavalry blanket thrown over it; in the other, a sheet hung from the ceiling. Behind it, partly hidden, was another, smaller cot and Blue guessed this was where Maddy slept.

Philo took a dented Civil War tin cup from a shelf and blew the dust out of it before setting it beside two enameled cups already on the table. He then grasped the coffeepot, cursing under his breath as it burned his hand, and quickly set it down beside the cups.

'What've I told you 'bout using a pot holder?' Maddy scolded her uncle.

Philo rolled his eyes at Blue and muttered something about certain young'uns being too smart for their britches.

Maddy ignored him, took a pot holder off a hook by the stove and sat across from Blue. 'Hope you like it black, Mr. Blue. It's the only way uncle and me drink it.'

'Black's fine,' he said.

Maddy waited for her uncle to join them, then picked up the coffeepot and filled the cups with black coffee that had the gummy viscosity of coal oil.

Blue took a sip and tried not to grimace at its sour bitterness.

'How come you ain't at the ranch tonight?' Maddy asked him.

'Mind your business, girl,' chided her uncle.

'It's all right,' Blue assured Philo. Then to Maddy: 'I don't work there anymore.'

'Since when?'

'Tonight.'

'What happened?'

'Girl,' Philo grumbled, 'quit questioning the man, y'hear?'

'But we're friends,' she protested. 'Friends are supposed to ask each other questions, uncle, else how can they know how they are? That's a fact.'

Stumped by her logic, Philo again rolled his eyes at Blue.

'Maddy,' Blue said quietly, 'there are several reasons why I quit, but what it boils down to is a matter of integrity.'

'I bet it had something to do with that hateful Mr. Logan,' she said darkly, 'didn't it?'

Philo sternly wagged his finger at her. 'One more peep out of you, girl, and it's off to the brig with you. Hear?'

Grumbling, Maddy obeyed her uncle and sat there sipping her coffee in silence.

'So I gather you'll be riding on now?' Philo said to Blue.

'Looks like, Colonel. Nothing to hold me here.'

Philo chewed on something before saying: 'Ever considered mining? There's a lot of gold *and* silver to be taken out of those hills.'

'I'm sure there is, sir. But handling horses is more to my liking than swinging a pick.'

'I don't blame you,' Philo said. 'It surely takes some getting used to.'

'Not to mention an aching back and hands full of blisters.'

'I'll not argue that, mister. But it's too bad just the same. I was fortunate enough to strike a rich vein of silver the other day and could sorely use help digging out the ore.'

Before Blue could reply, he heard horses approaching in the distance.

Philo heard them too. He jumped up and took the carbine down from the deer rack over the door. 'You best be going while you can,' he told Blue. 'We're about to have company and it isn't the friendly kind.'

'Gunmen wearing masks seldom are,' Blue said.

Philo looked surprised. 'You know about them, do you?'

Blue nodded. 'It's one of the reasons I quit the ranch.'

'Ah.'

'If it's okay with you, Colonel, I'd be honored to throw in with you.'

Philo quickly sized him up and then answered him by blowing out the kerosene lamp, plunging the cabin in darkness.

'Girl,' Philo told Maddy, 'get on the floor and stay there till this is over.'

'But, uncle — '

'Do as I say!' he ordered and Maddy reluctantly obeyed him.

By now Blue had opened the door. Winchester in hand, he stepped out into the darkness and looked in the direction of the oncoming horses.

Philo joined him, carbine in hand.

'How many you expecting?' Blue whispered.

Philo shrugged. 'Last time they hit us there were eight riders.'

'Sounds 'bout right,' Blue judged by the sound. 'Reckon I'll tie my horse up around back. If they figure they just got you and Maddy to contend with, I might be able to pick off three or four of them before they realize you ain't alone.'

'Sound military thinking,' Philo said. He ducked inside the cabin while Blue untied the pinto from the rail and led it around in back.

24

The riders were closing in fast.

From where he stood behind the cabin Blue guessed they were less than a hundred yards away. Quickly tying the pinto to the fence enclosing the hog pen, he hurried back to the front of the cabin and ducked behind the water trough. Waited.

Shortly, eight masked gunmen rode up, their horses sliding to a stop before the cabin.

The leader, a short cruel-faced man named Rufus Doyle, fired his rifle in the air. 'Old man!' he barked. 'Old man, get out here!'

Silence.

'We know you and the girl are in there! Better come out while you still can!'

The cabin door creaked open a few inches and Philo poked his carbine through the crack, saying: 'Unless you want blood spilled, ride on. All of you!'

Doyle gave a sneering laugh. 'That your final say?'

Before Philo could reply, another gunman said: 'Don't be a damn' fool, Colonel. If you don't leave now, we'll burn you out!'

'You want to see that little girl of yourn charred to a cinder?' Doyle threatened.

'This ain't Shiloh,' warned a third gunman. 'No Union troops to the rescue here.'

'He doesn't need any troops,' Blue said softly. Then as every gunman turned toward him in surprise: 'Mr. Winchester and Mr. Colt are all the help he needs.'

To emphasize his warning Blue fired at Doyle, the bullet knocking his hat off his head.

Startled, Doyle jerked back on the reins, causing his horse to rear up, almost throwing him. About him the horses of the other gunmen nickered and stirred nervously.

'Sorry to ruin a good hat,' Blue said. 'I was aiming at your ear.'

Doyle peered at the water trough, trying to pick out Blue in the darkness.

'Hold your fire, boys,' Philo said over his shoulder as if addressing other men. 'Our visitors are leaving.'

In the cabin, Maddy deliberately bumped into the table and knocked over a chair, making it seem as if there was more than one person hiding there.

Her ruse worked.

'Let's ride,' Doyle told his men. Then to Philo, 'You ain't seen the last of us, old man,' and digging in his spurs, rode away. The other gunmen followed and shortly the sound of galloping horses faded into the distance.

Blue stood up, had a moment of dizziness, and joined Philo at the cabin door.

'Well, we won that skirmish.'

'They'll be back, Colonel.'

'Tonight, you think?'

'If not, tomorrow, latest. And this

time they'll be no chasing 'em off. They won't leave till they've burned you out and maybe shot you and Maddy.'

'Sir, are you suggesting I run from the battlefield?'

'If you and Maddy want to stay alive, yeah.'

'Mr. Blue,' Philo said, standing erect and dignified, 'I've done some things in my life that I later regretted. But I've never ducked a fight and I don't intend to start now.'

'Not even for Maddy?'

'I was hoping she could go with you.'

'I ain't going anywhere,' Maddy said shrilly. 'Not without you, uncle. That's a fact.'

'You'll obey orders,' Philo snapped. 'And *that's* a fact!'

'Won't neither. And you can't make me go, uncle, 'cause you can't catch me.'

'I don't mean to interfere, Colonel,' Blue broke in. 'But as a former military man, didn't you ever order a tactical retreat?'

'Of course,' Philo said. 'Every commanding officer has. But that's not the same thing as running. Only cowards run, and — '

' "He who fights and runs away lives to fight another day," ' Blue quoted. 'Isn't that one of Robert E. Lee's favorite quotes? Or was it President Grant's?'

'I've no idea.'

'Doesn't really matter, anyway. Only reason I mentioned it was to point out that even the two most important generals in the War retreated at some time or other, and certainly no one ever called them cowards.'

Philo didn't answer right away. But his mind was racing and finally he said: 'What kind of tactical retreat do you have in mind, sir?'

'A hasty one,' said Blue. 'Pack up whatever you might need in an emergency and take Maddy up to the mine.' He paused, surprised to find himself getting involved, then added: 'Reckon the two of you'll be safer up in the hills. 'Least, for now.'

Philo grunted but didn't say anything as he mulled over Blue's advice.

'I'd be willing to help you build some kind of temporary shelter, Colonel.'

'Would you, now?'

'Naturally, after that I'd be moving on.'

'Naturally,' Philo said. He felt Maddy wriggle through the narrow doorway beside him and with a rare burst of warmth his arm about her. 'A man like you, he has to chase the wind.'

Maddy, surprised by her uncle's affection, said to Blue: 'We ain't asking you to help us for free, y'understand. You can have my share of the Lucky Lady — when uncle gives it to me, a course. That's a fact.'

At that moment the moon came from behind the clouds. In its silvery light Blue saw Maddy's unnaturally pale, pinkish-eyed albino face looking up at him with such trust, he felt guilty for even contemplating leaving.

'Seems to me,' he said, straight-faced,

'I remember a certain person saying that money wasn't why she was helping me. She was mighty emphatic 'bout it in fact.'

'That was different,' she protested. 'I was only showing you how to get to the Hotel Palomar. I wasn't building nothing or risking taking a bullet for you.'

'True enough,' Blue said. 'But a helping hand is a helping hand and one should be careful 'bout ignoring it. Tell you what,' he continued as Maddy looked undecided, 'let's see how things turn out and then we'll discuss the terms? Agreed?'

'Sounds fair,' Maddy said. Then to her uncle: 'Agreed?'

'Agreed,' he said, sticking out his hand. 'Let's shake on it like gentlemen.'

25

Dawn had broken by the time the three of them entered the hills. By then the pack-mule was laboring under the load on its back and Philo, knowing they still had a steep climb to reach the ridge ahead of them, suggested they rest when they reached the summit. 'From there to the mine isn't far,' he explained. 'It's just over the ridge, about halfway down the other is all.'

'Uncle uses the run-off from the creek to fill his sluices,' Maddy said as they rode on. 'That way he don't have to lug water up to the Lucky Lady.'

'How long you been digging in these hills?' Blue asked Philo.

'Years.' He took the long-stemmed clay pipe from his mouth and though there was no tobacco in the bowl, absently tapped it in the palm of his free hand. 'I first came here in the spring of '65, not long after I retired from the cavalry.'

'Why here?' Blue said. 'If you don't mind my asking?'

'My sister, Vera, suggested it,' Philo said. 'She and a shavetail who was stationed at Fort Apache had been courting. But when he was transferred to Texas, they broke up and she moved to Phoenix. A year or so later asked me to join her. She hadn't met Maddy's father yet and said she was feeling lonely, so I agreed.'

'But uncle didn't like living in a town,' Maddy put in. 'Too many people and laws he didn't agree with.'

'That was part of it,' agreed Philo. 'But also by then I'd gotten gold fever, so I picked up stakes and moved here, built the cabin and started panning.'

'How'd you do?' Blue asked.

'Fair to middling. I found a few nuggets and some dust, but nothing to write home about.'

'That wasn't your fault,' Maddy said supportively. 'It was on 'count of all the other prospectors panning in the creek 'longside you. Ain't that right?'

'They had something to do with it,' admitted Philo. 'But at the same time, in a strange way they were also responsible for my success.'

'How so?' inquired Blue.

'Well, they prodded me into wondering if there wasn't a better way to find gold. I mean all along I knew I'd never get rich fighting for every nugget or pinch of dust — there was too much competition. So I asked myself, what could I do about it? And that's when it hit me. I knew the gold didn't originate in the creek, which meant it had to come from somewhere else — somewhere above the creek. So I climbed up the hillside above where I'd been panning — where I'd found the biggest nuggets in fact — and started digging.'

'That was about the same time that momma got married and had me,' Maddy said, adding angrily: 'Which was the worst thing she could've done.'

'How do you mean?' Blue asked.

''Cause if she hadn't married pa, she wouldn't have been killed.'

'That's not true,' interrupted Philo.

''Tis too,' Maddy said. 'But for pa they wouldn't have been on that stage and then the Comanches couldn't have — '

'Enough!' Philo said. 'I've told you before, I won't have you blaming your father for something that wasn't his fault but was just a matter of fate. What Maddy's referring to,' he added to Blue, 'is that Vera's husband came from Bisbee and naturally he wanted his folks to meet his bride. So when Maddy was old enough, they left her with me and took the Overland stage — '

'Which was attacked by Comanches,' Maddy said bitterly.

'*Renegade* Comanches,' Philo corrected. 'A bunch of braves fired up by whisky who'd just gone off the reservation. Hardly something your father can be blamed for.'

'Maybe not in your eyes,' Maddy said stubbornly. 'But no matter how you sugar coat it, momma wouldn't have been killed if she hadn't been on that stage.'

Philo looked at Blue and shrugged hopelessly. 'Explain it to her,' he said. 'Maybe you'll have better luck than me.'

Blue would have sooner stuck his hand in a fire than get involved. But he heard himself say quietly: 'I'm real sorry 'bout your ma, Maddy. Losing someone you love is always tough, but it's doubly tough losing your ma. Even so, I got to tell you that I have to go along with your uncle on this. Painful as it is to accept, you can't run away from death. Not once it marks you. Whether you die from TB or pneumonia or a Comanche war arrow — or even fall downstairs and break your neck — it doesn't matter. Death doesn't care. Not so long as you die. And that's a fact, like you're always saying.'

Maddy didn't say anything for several moments. But Blue saw tears creep into her pink moonlike eyes and when she next spoke, there was no anger in her voice.

'I guess you're right. I guess it wasn't pa's fault. It's just . . . '

'Just what?' Blue said gently when she paused.

'I don't know . . . so . . . so unfair . . . ' Her voice cracked and tears spilled from her eyes.

Blue glanced at Philo and saw tears in his eyes, too.

'You've got that right,' he agreed. 'It is unfair, Maddy. 'Bout as unfair as it gets. But when adversity strikes, you just got to be brave and fight back.'

'How?'

'By telling yourself that your ma's in a better place and will always be there, waiting for you when it's your turn to go.'

'That's what uncle told me,' Maddy said, sniffing back her tears. 'So I reckon it must be true. Anyways,' she added, 'the good thing is I got to live out here with Uncle Philo and that beats living in dumb ol' Phoenix any day.'

They had reached the crest of the ridge. Dismounting, they gave the horses and the pack-mule a breather and drank thirstily from their canteens. In the pale yellow dawn-light the view was breathtaking. As far as Blue could see, a range of purple-brown hills stretched out before him, their peaks poking through a mist to form the distant horizon.

'There's the Lucky Lady,' Maddy said, pointing.

Blue followed her finger and saw several connecting sluice boxes descending from a mine entrance halfway down the rocky hillside below him. A steep winding trail led to the mine and then forked off to several other mines, all of which had been abandoned.

'Those other mines,' he asked Philo, 'are they yours?'

'No, sir. They were all dug by other miners who weren't as fortunate as me. Truth is,' he added, 'I was on the verge of quitting myself when I struck silver.' He shook his head in disbelief at the memory. 'Talk about serendipity. It was a small vein and I couldn't make up my mind whether to jump for joy or be disappointed. Before I could decide, I suddenly noticed something glinting in the same rock. Wondering what it was — I didn't dare think it was gold — I held my torch closer, and that's when I realized, by golly, it was indeed gold.'

'When you registered the claim, did the assayer tell you what quantity of gold there was in the ore?'

'Certainly. It was very high . . . close to ninety-eight percent.'

'What about the silver?'

'That was almost as high. That's why I was hoping you'd join forces with me and help me dig it out. I'd consider you a full partner,' he added. 'In other words, we'd split the profits three ways.'

'You, me and Maddy?'

'Exactly. Of course, that would only pertain to the silver or gold we found from now on. Anything I've already dug out would not be included.'

Blue had to admit it was tempting.

'Can I chew on it until tomorrow, Colonel? This would be a big change in plans for me and I don't want to jump into it without giving it some serious thought.'

'That's understandable.' Philo thought a moment before adding: 'How about forty-eight hours? Would that be enough time?'

'More than enough,' Blue said.

'Then let's get moving,' Philo said. 'I'd like to get some kind of temporary shelter erected as soon as possible.' He stepped up into the saddle, grasped the reins of the pack-mule and nudged his horse on down the slope.

Maddy beamed at Blue. 'Partners?' she exclaimed. 'Who would've ever figured?'

Blue didn't change expressions but chuckled to himself. He then swung up into the saddle and waited until Maddy had mounted before urging the pinto to follow her down the steep, winding trail that led to the mine.

26

Trees were scarce on the hillside but not in the ravine below. Years earlier Philo had chopped down some trees and removed the branches. He then had the mule drag the logs up to the mine entrance, where he used most of them to shore up the tunnel. The remaining logs he piled alongside the trail. Now, he and Blue used those logs to erect the walls of a temporary shelter. They then made a roof and a door-flap out of the two tarps they'd packed their gear in and covered the ground with their slickers. Lastly, they spread their blankets on top of the slickers, while Maddy found a small flat rock on which to set the coal-oil lamp.

'Reckon that'll do until you're finished digging out the ore,' Blue said as they stood back to admire their work. 'Or decide to build something more permanent.'

Philo nodded. 'I've slept in much worse when my regiment was bivouacked in Indian Territory,' he said reflectively.

'Me, too,' said Blue. 'Been times when if I wasn't being eaten alive by fire ants or buried by mud caused by flash floods, I considered myself a lucky man.'

'Want me to build a fire?' Maddy said. 'Boil some coffee?'

'No,' Philo said. 'Until we're sure we weren't followed, we'll make do with jerky and water.' He looked at Blue, who nodded in agreement. 'What you can do, though, is keep an eye out for riders while I show Mr. Blue the mine.'

'And if you do see riders,' added Blue, 'don't shoot at them. Come and get us as fast as you can.'

'Sure thing,' Maddy promised. Then to her uncle: 'Can I use your field glasses? That way, I'll be able to tell who they are while they're still a long ways off.'

Philo hesitated, about to refuse, and then grudgingly nodded. 'Handle them with great care, girl. They were a gift from — '

'Aunt Vera, yes, I know,' said Maddy. 'Don't worry, uncle, I'll guard 'em with my life.' She ducked inside the shelter and started rummaging in Philo's duffle bag.

'One thing you'll discover when you grow older,' Philo told Blue as they walked to the mine entrance, 'is that your possessions become more and more valuable to you — and inside your head a little voice keeps reminding you that once they're gone, they're gone forever. Then you've not only lost not the possession, which you may or may not consider a treasure, but you've also lost the memory that's attached to it.'

'I must already be old then,' Blue said wryly, 'because I feel that way now.'

Just inside the mine entrance a blackened wood torch was wedged into a crevice: Philo grasped it and handed it to Blue while he dug out a match. Lighting the oil-soaked grass wrapped around one end, Philo held the torch before him and led Blue along the narrow, shored-up tunnel. Both men had to duck down as they walked in order not to hit their heads on the low rounded ceiling. The tunnel was much longer than Blue expected and he soon felt sweat running down under his shirt as he fought back his claustrophobia.

'It may seem like a long way,' Philo said as if sensing Blue's suffering, 'but it isn't really — not when you consider how many years I've been digging. Probably no more than a few feet a day.'

Blue started to answer, heard himself slurring his words and fell silent. He and Philo continued on, bits of rock crunching underfoot, until they rounded a corner and there, a short distance ahead, Blue saw a wheelbarrow parked at the end of the tunnel. It was half-full of broken rock and leaned against it was a small box of dynamite and digging tools: a pick, shovel, sledgehammer.

As Philo and Blue reached the wheelbarrow the flickering torch illuminated the freshly-hammered wall beside it, and Blue glimpsed dull whitish-silver streaks and patches glinting on the surface.

'So that's what silver looks like when it's still in the rock?' he said. 'I would've walked right by it without ever knowing.'

Philo spoke with the pipe stem clamped between his teeth. 'Don't feel bad. At first I didn't know what it looked like either. I expected to find nuggets of silver, like you do when you're after gold, and must have missed lots of profitable veins over the years before an old prospector showed me what to look for. And thank heavens he did or I might still be searching. Unlike soldiering,' he added, 'there's no West Point or Virginia Military Academy to educate tenderfoots like me. I had to learn by my mistakes, and believe me,

Egan, I made more than my share!'

'Maybe so,' Blue said. 'But your perseverance finally paid off. And that's more than most miners can ever say.'

Back outside again they squinted in the bright morning sunlight and looked around for Maddy. She waved to them from the rocks above the shelter, hollering and pointing in the direction of the valley below.

Unable to understand what she was shouting, Philo signaled for her to come down.

She obeyed, field glasses hanging around her scrawny pale-skinned neck, a pile of loose dirt accompanying her she scrambled and slithered down the steep slope.

'R-Riders!' she exclaimed breathlessly.

'Logan's men?' Blue said.

'Yeah. Same ones who threatened to burn us out. What's more, they intend to kill us this time.'

'How do you know that?' her uncle asked.

''Cause they ain't wearing masks,' she said. 'Which means they don't care if we know who they are or not, since they plan on killing us anyway.'

'I hate to say it, Colonel,' Blue said, 'but I'm afraid she's right.'

Philo drew himself up to his full height and like an officer addressing his troops, said: 'Then by all means, gentlemen, let us give them a warm welcome!'

27

Expecting fierce resistance, the eight gunmen reined up and dismounted a safe distance from the mine entrance. Rifles in hand, they tied up their horses and took cover behind the rocks alongside the trail. From there they tried to see where Colonel Philo, Maddy and Blue were hiding.

When they couldn't, Doyle pointed at the makeshift shelter and told his men to drive out anyone who was hiding inside. The men started shooting, only stopping when they had emptied their rifles. Though they hadn't done much damage to the log walls, the door-flap was in tatters. The remaining shreds of canvas fluttered in the wind, allowing the men to see that the shelter was empty.

'They must be hiding in the mine,' Doyle said. 'Deutsch, Crocker, work your way over to the other side of the entrance. Make sure you get above it so you can see if anyone's inside the mine.'

The two gunmen started crawling toward the hill on the far side of the mine. They moved cautiously among the rocks, never allowing themselves to be targets, and shortly were in position. From there they peered over the rocks into the mine.

Soon Crocker signaled to Doyle that they couldn't see anyone. 'Too dark,' he yelled.

'Fire a few shots into the mine!' Doyle shouted back. 'Drive the bastards out.'

Crocker pumped his rifle to show he understood, then he and Deutsch opened fire. They stopped after a dozen or so shots and waited to see if anyone came running out.

Instead, something small was hurled at them from behind one of the rocks above the mine entrance. It twirled over and over in the air before landing on the dirt beside them.

The gunmen took one look at it, saw it was a stick of dynamite with a burning fuse, and with panicked yells scrambled away.

It was too late. They had only taken a few steps when the dynamite exploded.

The deafening explosion gutted the hillside, hurling tons of dirt and rocks into the air.

Alarmed, Doyle and the other gunmen dove for cover as debris rained down on them. But that wasn't the worst of it. Mixed in with the rocks and dirt were the bloody remains of Deutsch and Crocker.

Sickened, the gunmen jumped back from the gruesome body parts.

Doyle angrily yelled at them to take cover. But before they could, Blue and Philo tossed two more sticks of burning dynamite at them.

The explosions rocked the hillside. Huge chunks of it were hurled aloft; while at ground-level Doyle and the other gunmen were blown to pieces.

As the dust settled, Blue, Philo and Maddy stood up from behind the rocks, ready to shoot anyone that moved. No one did.

'Reckon it's all clear,' Blue said.

Philo indicated the stick of dynamite he was holding. 'D'you think we should make sure?'

Blue shook his head. 'Let's not press our luck, Colonel. We don't want to risk starting a landslide that could kill us all.'

'No, no, of course not.'

'But just to be on the safe side, you stay here with Maddy while I go take a looksee.'

'I appreciate your noble offer,' Philo said. 'But I insist on going with you, sir.'

'We'll all go,' said Maddy. Before they could stop her, she scrambled down between the rocks ahead of them.

'Just like her mother,' Philo exclaimed, his tone a mixture of irritation and admiration. 'Impetuous to a fault!' He quickly followed Maddy.

'With a touch of her uncle thrown in,' Blue thought aloud. Rifle in the

crook of his arm, he slowly made his
way down the rocky slope after the
colonel.

28

The three of them searched the hillside below the mine, but all they found were the gory remains of the dead gunmen.

'I suppose we're morally obliged to bury them,' Philo said to Blue.

'I don't know 'bout morally, Colonel, but unless we want to be eaten alive by ants and flies, I think it's definitely a good idea.'

'Consider it done, sir,' said Philo. Then as it hit him: 'Did you say 'we'?'

'I did.'

Maddy instantly perked up. 'Does that mean you're going to stay and help us?'

'For a mite longer maybe. Unless you can think of a reason I shouldn't?'

'Not me,' Maddy said, barely able to believe her good fortune. 'Heck, I want you here more than anything!'

'Then it's settled, sir,' Philo said.

'Not quite,' Blue said. 'Before we can officially become partners, Colonel, there's something I got to take care of.'

'Hunt Logan?'

Blue nodded.

'But why?' Maddy broke in. 'Without his gunmen, he ain't no threat to us?'

'He'll always be a threat,' Blue said. 'Man like him, he'll never be happy until he owns the whole valley and there's no one left to challenge him.'

'Meaning you?'

'Meaning me.'

'But, why?' Maddy said. 'You ain't a farmer or a squatter. Why do you care who controls the valley?'

'Someone's got to,' Blue said, thinking that he had to do it right away, while he was still capable of it.

'Then let the sheriff or the marshal handle it. That's what they get paid for.'

'Maddy's right,' agreed Philo. 'Stay here with us, Egan, and I promise you'll end up with more money than you ever dreamed of.'

''Sides, if you're rich,' Maddy said,

'then you won't have to kill folks to make a living. Please,' she begged when he didn't reply. 'I don't want you to kill people anymore. Not even men who deserve to die.'

'Why not?' Blue said. 'Would you sooner they lived and went on hurting folks?'

'No. That ain't right neither. All I'm saying is I don't want you pulling the trigger. 'Specially when it comes to Hunt Logan. He may be mean and greedy, but that don't mean he deserves to die.'

'There, I disagree with you.'

'Yeah, and I bet I know why.'

'Meaning?'

'Meaning you want what he's got.'

'What — the Darby spread? You couldn't be more wrong.'

'I wasn't talking 'bout the ranch. I meant Miss Hilly.'

'Watch your mouth,' Blue warned.

'That's what this is all about, ain't it?' Maddy continued. 'You loving her and Logan being in your way?'

'Girl,' Philo cautioned, 'you're treading on awful thin ice.'

Ignoring her uncle, she said to Blue: 'You can deny it all you want, but — '

'I'm not denying it,' he said, cutting her off. 'What I'm denying is that I plan on killing Logan to get Hilly. That's not true.'

'But you do want her?' Philo said, curious. 'For your wife, I mean?'

'If it was purely up to me, Colonel, yes.'

Philo sighed, disappointed. 'Then I doubt if we can be partners, sir. Much as I would like that, no man can be in two places at once. The partner I'm looking for has to be fully committed to the Lucky Lady.'

'I understand,' Blue said. 'But you did give me forty-eight hours to decide, Colonel. If I leave now, that should be more than enough time for me to get the answers I need. That's unless you've changed your mind?'

'Not at all,' Philo said. 'I'll even give

you more time if you think you'll need it.'

Blue shook his head. 'Thanks, but a deal's a deal.' He turned to leave then stopped, looked back and said: 'Oh, and no matter what the outcome is, Colonel, I'll be back to give you my answer face-to-face.'

'We'll be here,' Philo said, adding: 'Won't we, Maddy?'

She nodded, so close to tears that she didn't dare answer.

'Fair enough,' Blue said. 'Then let's get to burying what's left of the dead 'fore the sun makes the flesh too ripe to handle.'

29

It was late afternoon when Blue rode under the wooden arch that welcomed everyone to the Sundown Ranch. Reining in the sweat-caked pinto, he rested his rifle across the saddle horn and warily looked about him. The large open area fronting the barn, corrals and the ranch-house was deserted. Not even Ramirez, an old Mexican who'd worked at the ranch since childhood, was around. The only sign of life Blue could see were four sleepy-looking horses huddled together in the main corral. He recognized two of them: Hilly's black thoroughbred and Logan's dappled gray stallion.

Wondering where Logan was and if he'd gotten word yet that the gunmen he'd hired were all dead, Blue nudged the pinto forward and rode slowly up to the house. As he dismounted and tied up his horse, he heard Logan and Hilly arguing inside. Tucking his rifle into its scabbard, he listened briefly but couldn't make out what they were saying. But whatever it was, Logan was growing louder and angrier by the moment.

Deciding not to let them know he was here, Blue removed his spurs and put them in his saddlebag. Then drawing his .44, he spun the cylinder to make sure the hammer wouldn't fall on an empty chamber, re-holstered the gun and quietly entered the house.

Hilly was now the only one speaking and Blue let her voice lead him into the parlor and on, across the room to the door of her office. There he paused in the doorway.

Logan had his back to him, fists clenched at his sides, the width of his body blocking Blue's view of Hilly. Yet somehow, even as Logan listened to her telling him to leave, he sensed someone was behind him and whirled around, hand reaching for his six-gun.

It was a mistake. Before Logan's gun even cleared leather, he found himself looking at the wrong end of Blue's .44 and quickly raised both hands.

'You're my witness,' he told Hilly.

'To what?'

'That I didn't provoke this hired killer. If he shoots me, it's murder plain and simple.'

'I ain't going to shoot you,' Blue said, 'though I sure as hell ought to.'

'Then why're you here?'

'To let you know that the gunmen you hired to drive folks out of this valley are dead. Every last one of them.'

Logan paled. 'You're bluffing, damn you. Not even you could gun down all of them.'

'I had help,' Blue said. 'But any way you cut it, you're on your own now. Unless, of course,' he added to Hilly, 'you were behind this weasel all along?'

'Is that what you think of me?' she said, stung. 'That I could actually stoop to his level?'

'You're marrying him,' Blue reminded.

'What else am I supposed to think?'

'Not anymore,' she replied, holding up the finger that once wore Logan's engagement ring. 'I just broke off our engagement. That's what we were arguing about. As for what you think of me,' she added, 'I can't change that. I'd like to think that you trusted me enough to believe what I'm saying is true, but if you don't — well, so be it. Guess I'll have to live with that.'

Blue looked at her, deep into her large hazel eyes and saw nothing but honesty staring back at him.

'I believe you,' he said.

'Thank you.'

'But that don't change anything 'tween us,' Blue growled at Logan. 'You're a lying, gutless sidewinder who's got just two choices: ride out of this valley now or be buried here. Your call.' He returned his gun to the holster, got ready to draw and waited for Logan's response.

Logan gave an ugly sneering laugh. 'You'd like me to draw down on you, wouldn't you? That way you could kill me legally, take over my job and try to worm your way into Hilly's heart. Well, I'm not going to make it that easy for you. Or for you,' he said to Hilly. 'I'll leave the valley but believe me, sure as winter follows fall, I'll be back. And when I do it'll be with enough men to help me collect what's mine. Trust me on that.' He pushed past Blue and crossed the parlor to the door leading out into the entrance hall. There he paused and looked back at Hilly, saying: 'Oh, and just so you know. Your stepdad — the man you worshipped and thought could do no wrong — didn't die of natural causes like Doc Ahearn thought. He was suffocated.'

'W-What're you talking about?' Hilly said, shaken. 'How do you know that?'

'I hear things.'

'Like, what?'

'That someone held a pillow over Owen's face while he was asleep. And that he struggled and whimpered like a baby 'fore he died.'

For one long moment Hilly stared at Logan with absolute horror and hatred.

Blue eyed him grimly. 'This 'someone' — that wouldn't be you by any chance?'

'Me?' Logan said mockingly. 'Why would I kill my benefactor?'

'Maybe because he found out you shot Sheriff Colton?'

'That's a lie!' Logan said. 'Colton committed suicide just like I told you. And that's the God's honest truth!'

For the first time he sounded sincere. 'Okay,' Blue said, 'for the moment, let's say that's true. There's still a little matter of rustling to be cleared up. Owen must've stumbled onto the fact that you were behind it and threatened to expose you. For that you killed him.'

Logan gave a sneering laugh. 'You make me sick. Even if that was true, who'd ever believe you, a wanted gunman, over me? Hell, everyone knows Owen treated me like a son and encouraged me to marry his daughter,

so how could I do such a despi-
cable — '

A sudden single gunshot cut off his
words.

Logan staggered back, eyes wide with
shocked disbelief, a red stain seeping
through his shirt. Then he crumpled to
the carpet, dead.

Blue, equally shocked, turned and
saw Hilly holding his smoking gun. He
tried to take it back from her. But she
fought him, twisting and jerking until
she finally broke free.

'Dammit, Hilly,' Blue said angrily,
'give me my gun!'

'No, no, you're not going to take the
blame for this. I knew exactly what I
was doing when I grabbed it out of the
holster! And that's what I'll tell the
judge!'

'You can tell all the judges in the
territory, but none of them will believe
you. They'll just figure you're covering
up for me, a hired gun, and add another
knot to the hangman's rope.'

'Then I'll keep talking until they do

believe,' she said tearfully.

'Hilly, please — '

'No! I'm not going to let you take the fall for a murder you didn't commit.'

'Sure you are,' Blue said gently. 'I ain't trying to be noble or dramatic, but my life's already over . . . while yours is just beginning. Not only that, but if you admit to killing Logan, a man who at best was worthless, you'd be destroying your stepfather's dreams. I never met Owen unfortunately, but I've known men like him, good men, and I know he built this spread for you and the children that you're going to have and raise.'

Hilly, eyes still full of tears, didn't answer.

'You can see that now, can't you?'

Again, Hilly didn't answer.

Blue stepped close and gently pried his gun from her hand. Holstered it.

His touch dragged Hilly back to reality. She looked at Logan's corpse as if seeing it for the first time. 'Oh dear God,' she wept. 'What've I done?'

'Nothing that didn't deserve to be

done,' Blue assured her. 'So rest easy, knowing you've made the world a better place.' He leaned close and kissed her on the forehead. 'Be seeing you, Miss Hilly.'

'W-Where're you going?'

'To bury the evidence.' He picked up Logan's corpse, effortlessly slung it over his shoulder and crossed the parlor to the outer door.

'Egan,' she said through her tears. 'Wait.'

Then as Blue turned and looked at her:

'You don't have to leave. You could bury him on the ranch.'

'If I did that, you'd never be rid of him. Or me.'

'Maybe that's what I'm hoping for,' she whispered.

He knew the feeling too well. But he wasn't about to saddle her with a husband only a heartbeat from the grave. So he just smiled sadly.

'I suppose it's too late to ask you to stay?'

'Reckon so, Miss Hilly.'

'What a shame,' she said. 'What a waste.'

'I wouldn't say that,' Blue said softly. 'From now on, no matter where I go, just the thought of you will keep me warm on wintry nights. And that's more than any hired gun deserves.' Though it was the toughest thing he'd ever had to do, he tipped his hat and walked out.

Moments later Hilly heard the front door slam after him.

She knew then she'd lost him.

If she'd been stabbed in the heart it could not have hurt more.

MCANDREW'S STAND

Bill Cartright

Jenny McAndrew and her two sons live in the valley known as McAndrew's Pass. When they hear that the new Rocky Mountains Railroad Company has plans to lay a line through the valley — and their farm — they are devastated at the prospect of their simple lives being destroyed. Clarence Harper, the ruthless boss of the railroad company, is not a man to brook opposition. But in the McAndrews, he finds one family that will not be bullied into submission . . .

THE ROBIN HOOD OF THE RANGE

James Clay

Ricky Cates is a vicious outlaw who kills without remorse. He also has a talent for deception, having convinced a local writer that he's the Robin Hood of the Range: a man who takes from the rich and gives to the poor. Rance Dehner is on Cates's blood-spattered trail. But before he can reach his target, he must confront Cates's henchmen, another detective obsessed with catching the killer — and a young woman who is hopelessly and dangerously in love with this Robin Hood . . .